CHRISTIANA'S JOURNEY

Special Prize

Presented to

Jonathan Reid
For Attendance
Larne Bible Presbyterian
Church Sabbath
School 1986

STEWART McELHERAN CO., 66/70 Mill Street, Ballymena

CHRISTIANA'S JOURNEY

A Victorian Children's Story based on John Bunyan's PILGRIM'S PROGRESS   Part 2

BRIDGE PUBLISHING, INC.

Publishers of:

LOGOS • HAVEN • OPEN SCROLL

CHRISTIANA'S JOURNEY
Copyright © 1982 this revised edition by Christopher Wright
All rights reserved
Printed in the United States of America
Library of Congress Catalog Number: 82-70860
International Standard Book Number: 0-88270-533-4
Bridge Publishing, Inc.
South Plainfield, New Jersey 07080

Other children's classics revised and updated by
Christopher Wright:

Christie's Old Organ by Mrs. O.F. Walton
Young Christian's Pilgrimage by John Bunyan
A Peep Behind the Scenes by Mrs. O.F. Walton
Target Earth! by John Bunyan

Contents

Introduction to *Christiana's Journey*

John Bunyan's *Pilgrim's Progress* is very well
known. Not quite so well known is the second part of
his story about Christiana. One hundred years ago
Helen L. Taylor decided to rewrite both the story of
Christian and the story of Christiana specially for
children. Although some of the words and way of
telling the story are out of date now, I think that Helen
Taylor wrote two books that deserve to be brought out
in a new edition.

It has been quite hard work carefully revising Helen
Taylor's books, but I have really enjoyed the time spent
on them. This book, *Christiana's Journey,* is based on
the second part of *Pilgrim's Progress,* but it can be read
before the first part (which I have now called *Young
Christian's Pilgrimage*). In this book, Christiana sets
out to make the journey that Christian has already
made. John Bunyan says that *Pilgrim's Progress* came
to him as a dream, with our lives seeming like a
journey. We all make that journey through life, but not
everyone is on the same road!

If you enjoy reading *Christiana's Journey* and *Young
Christian's Pilgrimage* as much as I have done while
revising them, you will have read two books to
remember for the rest of your life!

—Christopher Wright

CHRISTIANA'S JOURNEY

CHRISTIANA'S JOURNEY

CHAPTER 1

A Letter from the King

Christiana sat on the hill with her three brothers and small sister. Far below them the people in the city went about their work. Christiana liked to sit high up like this above the City of Destruction. Many times she had sat here with Christian—before he had gone on his journey.

Christiana often thought about that journey which her friend had made from the City of Destruction. She wondered what sort of city Christian now lived in. The Heavenly City, some called it. Had he really reached it? Or had he been lost in the Dark River?

Christiana had often heard about the Heavenly City. People said her own father and mother were both living there. While they had been travelling to it along the Way of the King, they had given many loving messages to Christiana, begging her to begin her journey, and bring her brothers and young sister with her. But, not very long before her friend Christian went away, she was told that her father had crossed the Dark River to the Heavenly City. Then, in a few days, her mother followed him. Christiana had no more messages from them, and she felt sad and lonely.

Christian had often talked to her about his Book and

she had listened to him, but she did not believe what he said. "If my father and mother are really living in a beautiful city like that," she used to say, "I am sure they would not forget us. They would have sent me another message. I think they were lost in the Dark River, and we shall never see them any more!"

Then young Christian went away, and Christiana feared that he would be lost too, and she could not help being worried as she thought of it.

The summer and autumn passed, and the winter also. Then the spring came round again, and so Christiana took her young sister Innocence up this hill to gather flowers.

"Last year," she thought, "Christian came with us up this very hill, the day before he went away, and we talked together. I wonder if he *has* found the Heavenly City, or whether he has been lost."

Christiana looked across the open fields, and she could see a light in the distance, shining brightly. Christian had told her there was a Gate there, where pilgrims must start out for the Heavenly City. "Perhaps," she said to herself, "I will start out some day; but I must wait until Innocence is a little older. And I could not leave my brothers by themselves; I am sure they would not go with me now." Then she lifted Innocence in her arms, and turned back towards the City of Destruction.

In the evening, when she had put Innocence to bed, the house was quite still, for the boys were playing in the streets with their friends. Christiana sat down by the fire and thought of her father and mother, and of

A Letter from the King

Christian also. She wished very much that she could see them all once more. That night she had a strange dream. She fancied she had really found the Heavenly City, and that she was walking along its streets with Christian. Innocence was there too, and her three brothers, and they all went together into a beautiful palace, where the King Himself met them, and spoke to them.

"I wish it had been true, and not a dream!" she thought, when she awoke; and as she could not go to sleep again she got up, although it was very early, and began to tidy the house. Presently she heard a knock at the door, and went out to see who was calling.

She expected to see a neighbor, but a visitor to the city stood in the road. Her name was Wisdom, and she was the daughter of Evangelist. Christiana knew her, for she had seen her in the city, and had sometimes watched her calling the children round her that she might talk to them about the King.

"I have been wishing to speak to you," she said, "but I have not been able to find you in the streets lately."

"No," replied Christiana sitting with Innocence in her arms, "I was tired of the streets, and I took my little sister up the hill."

Wisdom laid her hand upon the girl's shoulder. "I don't think you are very happy, Christiana."

"I am lonely," she answered.

"Yet you have your three brothers, and Innocence."

"Yes, but I am lonely," Christiana repeated. "My father and mother are gone, and so is Christian, and I

3

"I am lonely," Christiana answered.

A Letter from the King

do not know what has become of them."

"They are with the King, in His glorious City."

"Ah!" said Christiana, "but I have been told so often that the stories about the King and the Heavenly City are not true."

"They really are true," replied Wisdom. "The King is sorry that you do not believe them, and He has sent me to tell you that He wishes you to begin your journey at once, and to bring the boys and Innocence with you."

"So many of us?" exclaimed Christiana.

"Yes. The King's City is large, and there is room in it for every pilgrim who comes to its gates. Do you not know how pleased your family will be when they hear that those gates have been opened for *you?*"

A tear came into Christiana's eyes, but she wiped it away. "I will think about it," she said, looking away from Wisdom.

"This will help you," answered Wisdom, and she drew out a folded paper. "It is a letter from the King. Keep it safely and read it often, and when you reach the Heavenly City, show it to the angels who will meet you at the gate, for it is a promise to you from the King."

CHAPTER 2

Christiana Shows the Letter to Her Brothers

Christiana could scarcely believe that the letter was really from the King, and for her: yet, when she had read it, her heart was filled with joy and sorrow together—joy that the King should send her such a loving message, and sorrow that she had not learned to love and obey Him before.

Christiana looked up again at Wisdom, who was standing near her. "I will go," she said, "and I will try to take the children with me."

Wisdom smiled at her. "That is right," she said, "do not wait any longer. The way is easier for children than it is for older people, and the King will help you in all your difficulties."

"Can you not go with us?" said Christiana, "I should not be frightened if you showed us the way."

"No; I have other work to do. But you need not be frightened. You know the way to the Gate to the King's Way, and when you have passed through it, you will meet with many of the King's servants, who will help you."

Christiana read the King's letter many times that day, and in the evening she showed it to Matthew, her eldest brother. "What shall I do?" she asked him.

7

"Do you think it *really* came from the King?"

Christiana Shows the Letter to Her Brothers

"You will go—will you not?"

"I should like to go, and take Innocence; but what will become of you boys if I leave you alone?"

"We must go too," said Matthew; "at any rate *I* will."

"Will you really? Oh, I am so glad!"

"I have often thought about it," continued Matthew, "since we knew that our father and mother had crossed the Dark River. When Christian and Faithful went away, I was half inclined to follow them. It will be nice now for us all to go together."

Christiana smiled as she looked into the fire. "Mother would be so pleased to see us! But I do not know whether James and Joseph will come. Perhaps they will be afraid of the long journey."

Just at that moment the door opened, and the two younger boys ran in. "Oh!" exclaimed James, "we are *so* tired! What are you talking about, you two?"

"Christiana has had a letter," replied Matthew; and he laid the paper on the table, where his brothers could read it as they stood side by side.

"It is from the King!" said Joseph. "Why has He written to Christiana?"

"Who brought it?" asked James. "Do you think it *really* came from the King?"

"One of the strangers brought it. Her name is Wisdom. You have often seen her in the streets."

"I know her. She spoke to me one day, and I liked her. Will you go?" Joseph came round to the fire, and leaned against his sister's chair, looking into her face.

"Will you come with me, Joseph?" asked Christiana.

"I don't mind. Shall we have to fight anybody? Will there be any wild beasts?"

"I do not know, but Wisdom said we need not be frightened; the King will take care of us."

"I should like to be a pilgrim," said James; "but Innocence is so small, and you can't leave *her* behind."

"No," said Matthew, "of course not. She can walk a little, and we must carry her when she is tired."

"When shall we go?" asked Joseph. "We have to pass through that Gate with the lamp over it, haven't we? Oh, don't you remember? Pliable went with Christian last spring, and *they* fell into the Slough!"

"Then *we* will be careful!" said Matthew. "When can we be ready, Christiana? Tomorrow?"

"The next day, I think. We can prepare everything at night, and then start very early, as soon as the gates of our city are opened."

CHAPTER 3

The Children Leave the City of Destruction

In the afternoon of Christiana's last day in the City of Destruction, three or four girls came in to see her. Christiana knew one of them well. Her name was Mercy.

"Oh, you *do* look busy!" cried one. "We came to ask you to go with us into the country tomorrow."

"I don't think I can," replied Christiana.

"Why, you are putting everything away!" exclaimed another. "You must be getting ready for a journey!"

Christiana had not meant to say anything about the King's letter, but now she felt that it would be better to tell her friends what she intended to do.

"I have had a message from the King," she said; "and I am going to the Heavenly City."

"Oh," cried the girls, "how *can* you be so foolish!"

"*I* am not foolish. I wish you would all come with me!"

"And leave our beautiful city and all our friends! What will your poor little sister do, and the boys? It is very wrong of you, Christiana, to think of leaving them."

"They are going with me."

Then the girls laughed. "You must be mad! How can

11

a child like Innocence be a pilgrim? Just think of all we
have heard about your friend Christian and his troubles.
He was nearly lost in the Slough to begin with, and you
know when Mistrust and Timorous came back, they
told us that he had met with *lions* on the Hill
Difficulty!"

"Yes," said another, "and you cannot have forgotten
the news we had from Vanity Fair about the death of
Faithful. You are a silly girl to run into such danger,
especially when you have a baby sister and three
brothers to take care of."

"Matthew is old enough now to take care of me,"
replied Christiana; "and we are not afraid. The King
has promised to watch over us. Here is His letter. You
can read it if you like."

But the girls did not believe in the King, or care
about His messages. "It is of no use wasting our time,"
they said. "You must do as you please, but you will soon
wish yourself back again!"

Christiana was not sorry when the door closed, and
she was once more alone. "I am glad Wisdom came to
me," she said to herself, "for I should have thought just
as my friends do, if she had not spoken to me."

Matthew did not stay out for long in the city that day,
and even James and Joseph were eager to begin their
pilgrimage. They came home early, so that they might
help Christiana.

"I have washed your clothes and mended them," she
said; "but I never noticed before how shabby they were
getting. You must keep them as tidy as you can, and

perhaps the King will send us some new ones."

Very early in the morning the children went quietly away from their cottage, and passed out at the gate of the city. The gatekeeper did not stop them, for he thought they were only going to spend a long day in the meadows. Christiana carried Innocence in her arms, and Matthew had brought a bag with some food. James and Joseph ran on before them, for they were anxious to reach the Gate to the King's Way.

"Perhaps we shall meet a lion," said Joseph; "but I shall not be frightened!"

"Oh, no!" said James; "pilgrims are *always* brave, and, of course, we must fight for our sisters!"

Innocence clapped her small hands when she saw the white heads of the daisies in the grass. Matthew began to gather a few of them for her to carry. While he was doing this a girl came in sight, walking quickly across the meadow from the city.

"Stop!" she cried. *"Please* let me speak to Christiana!"

Christiana looked round. "It is Mercy," she said.

Mercy was out of breath, but she caught Christiana's hand and held it fast. "I didn't like to go with the other girls," she said. "May I walk a little way with you?"

"Oh, yes!" replied Christiana. "Will you not go *all* the way?"

"I have had no message," said Mercy, as she thought of the King's letter to Christiana, which she and her friends had laughed at earlier.

"That will not matter," said Matthew. "I am sure I have heard Evangelist say that the King would like *all*

"Please let me speak to Christiana!"

the children to become pilgrims."

But Mercy shook her head. She feared that the King might not receive her if she came to His City without being sent for.

"I will tell you what to do," said Christiana. "Come with us as far as the Gate, and we will ask the King's servant to let you pass through."

Mercy was willing to do this, and the boys were glad to have her with them, so they all went on together very happily until they reached the edge of the Slough of Despair.

"This is where Pliable and Christian were nearly drowned," said Christiana. "I do not know how we shall cross, for it seems very dangerous indeed."

The soft green mud was oozing between the tufts of grass; but as they looked carefully round, the children caught sight of stepping-stones. James and Joseph skipped lightly from stone to stone; but Matthew held Mercy's arm, for she was afraid of falling; and Innocence clasped her hands tightly round Christiana's neck. Soon they found themselves once more on firm ground, and they knew that no other unsafe place lay between them and the Gate to the King's Way.

"We will walk quickly," said Christiana, "while the day is cool and pleasant, and perhaps we may be allowed to rest a little when we have entered the Way of the King."

CHAPTER 4

At the Gate

About the middle of the day the six pilgrims came up to the Gate. It was a strong door set in the high stone wall. Over it were the words: "Knock, and the door will be opened to you." The bright light, which the children had seen in the distance shone on these words which the Prince had put there Himself.

"You are the eldest," said Matthew to Christiana, "and the King's letter was for you, so you had better knock, and tell the keeper why we have come."

Christiana knocked at the Gate in the high wall several times, but no one answered. Then a dog began to bark very furiously indeed, and although James and Joseph had meant to be brave, they both turned pale and whispered to Mercy, "Shall we go home?"

"Oh, no!" said Mercy; but she felt frightened also.

"We must knock again," said Matthew; so Christiana lifted the knocker, and rapped once more as loudly as she could.

Then Goodwill, who kept the Gate, came out of his cottage and asked, "Who is there?" and when the dog heard his voice it left off barking.

"Please do not be annoyed with us, because we knocked so often," said Christiana. "We thought you did not hear us, and we were frightened of the dog."

Goodwill looked kindly at the children, and asked, "Where do you come from? And what do you wish me to do for you?"

"We have come from the city where Christian lived, and we are going to be the King's pilgrims if you will let us pass through the Gate. These are my brothers, and this is my little sister."

Then Goodwill took Christiana's hand, and led her through the Gateway, saying, "Let the children come to me."

Christiana knew that these words had been spoken by the Prince Himself. She had seen them written in the old Book of which Christian had been so fond, and she felt very happy as she entered the Way of the King with Innocence in her arms, and all her brothers by her side.

Poor Mercy had not dared to follow her friends. She drew back when the Gate was opened, and Goodwill did not see her. Then, as she heard the Gate close and found herself alone, she began to cry out, for she thought that perhaps Christiana would forget her. But Christiana had not forgotten her.

"We have a friend with us," she said to Goodwill. "She wishes to go to the Heavenly City. The King has not sent her a letter, so she is afraid—"

Christiana had not time to say anything more, for Mercy had grown frightened, and was knocking upon the Gate with all her might.

"Who is that?" said Goodwill, and Christiana answered

that it must be Mercy. So Goodwill opened the Gate again and looked out.

Mercy was not strong, and the fear of being left behind had made her feel faint. After knocking at the Gate she had fallen upon the grass, and could not even look up when she heard the voice of Goodwill.

The old man stooped down and lifted Mercy to her feet. "Do not be frightened," he said; and then Mercy opened her eyes. "Tell me why you have come," said Goodwill gently.

"Oh," said Mercy, "I had no letter! It was only Christiana who asked me."

"Did she ask you to go to the Heavenly City with her?"

"Yes, and I should like to go. Will the King be angry, or will He let me be a pilgrim?"

"The King's Gate is open to *everyone* who knocks at it. Look at the promise written above," said Goodwill. "Come in with me, and do not worry any more."

Then he led Mercy also through the Gateway, and he gave her some sweet-scented herbs to smell, so that she did not feel faint any more.

CHAPTER 5

The Beginning of the Pilgrimage

"You must rest in my cottage for a while," said Goodwill; and he brought the children into a cool, quiet room, where he told them to stay until he came for them later.

"Oh," exclaimed Christiana, when they were alone, "how glad I am that we are all here!"

"I think *I* ought to be more glad than any of you!" said Mercy.

"I was so afraid," continued Christiana. "When we knocked, nobody answered us. I thought perhaps we had had our long walk for nothing, especially when that dog barked so dreadfully."

"The worst time was when *you* were all gone in," said Mercy, "and *I* was left behind. I didn't like to knock again, until I looked up, and saw the words carved over the Gateway. Then I knocked as hard as I could!"

Christiana smiled. "You *did* knock!" she said; "I thought you meant to force the Gate open!"

"Well," said Mercy, "I couldn't help it. The Gate was shut, and that fierce dog must have been somewhere near. *You* would have knocked loudly if you had felt so frightened! Was Goodwill angry? What did he say?"

"He was smiling. I don't think he was angry. But I

21

wonder why he keeps that dog! If I had known about it, I am not sure whether I should have dared to come. However, we are safe now, and I am very glad indeed."

"So am I," said Mercy. "I think I will ask Goodwill why he allows such a savage dog to be near the Gate."

"Yes," said James; "do ask him, Mercy! We are afraid it will bite us when we leave here!"

So when Goodwill returned, Mercy asked him why he kept the dog.

"It is not mine," he answered. "There is a great castle not far from this gate, which belongs to the Wicked Prince. The dog lives at the castle, but he can run along his master's ground until he comes close to my cottage. Then, when he hears the pilgrims knocking, he begins to bark. The Wicked Prince has taught him to do this; and once or twice he has broken through the fence, and has bitten a pilgrim. But I always open the Gate as quickly as possible, and you know the King's servants must not let themselves be frightened when danger is near to them."

He laid his hand on Mercy's head, and the girl looked up at him. "It was wrong of me," she said. "Another time I will remember, and trust the King to take care of me."

Then Christiana began to ask Goodwill about the King's Way, and he was ready to answer all her questions. Afterwards he told the pilgrims to wash themselves, while he prepared a comfortable meal for them. At last they felt rested and refreshed, and able to go on their journey.

Matthew began to gather the ripe berries.

Christiana's Journey

The garden of the Wicked Prince's castle lay close to the King's Way, but a high wall had been built by the King's servants along the roadside, so that the savage dog could not see the pilgrims or come near to hurt them after they had passed through the Gate. A number of trees were planted in the garden, and their branches hung over the wall and made a pleasant shade. Christiana did not realize that the garden belonged to the castle, and she allowed the children to walk near this wall. Presently they saw that some of the trees were full of fruit, and as the branches were within easy reach, Matthew began to gather the ripe berries.

"You should not do that," said Christiana. "The fruit is not ours, and perhaps those berries are not safe to eat."

"They are very sweet and nice!"

"I would not eat them if I were you."

James and Joseph were wise enough to listen to their sister, and they threw away the berries which Matthew had gathered for them; but Matthew felt vexed, and said to himself, "I am nearly as old as Chistiana, and I know quite as much as she does. The fruit is very good!" So he went on eating.

CHAPTER 6

The First Trouble

The children had not gone far from the Gate when they saw two boys coming toward them. These boys were much taller than Matthew; their clothes were of bright-colored velvet, and they wore caps with little plumes fastened at the side.

"They must be princes," said Joseph. "Has the King sent them to meet us?"

"I don't think the King's servants are ever dressed in such a way," replied Christiana; "and I am sure they cannot be princes from the Heavenly City, for their faces are bad and ugly. Let us walk quickly, and take no notice of them."

The two boys were laughing and talking together, and when Christiana and the children came near to them they stood in the middle of the path, and would not allow the pilgrims to pass by. Matthew and his brothers were frightened, and Christiana scarcely knew what to do.

"We have no money to give you," she said. "We are quite poor children, and we are going to the King's City."

Then the tallest boy seized Christiana's hand, and his companion caught hold of Mercy. "Don't be

25

frightened," they said; "we don't want your money, and we are not going to hurt you. You are two very pretty girls, and you shall stay and talk to us for a little while."

"We cannot," said Christiana; "we have no time to spare. *Please* let us go on!"

"Oh, that is all nonsense!" replied the boys. "We shall not let you waste a lovely day like this in traveling. Do not say you will not stay with us, because we shall *make* you stay!"

Perhaps if Matthew had not been eating the fruit from the Wicked Prince's garden he would have felt brave, and would, at least, have *tried* to defend his sisters and Mercy; but he only stood full of fear. When James and Joseph saw him they were frightened also, and clung closely to him.

Christiana and Mercy saw that they would not be able to get safely away from these two boys, so they both called out for help. As they were not very far from the gate, Goodwill heard them, and sent a man at once to see what had happened.

The man ran quickly, and soon caught up with the children. As he drew near he called to the boys, saying, "What are you doing? How is it that you dare to hinder the King's pilgrims?"

When the boys heard the man's voice, they let Christiana and Mercy go free, and hurried to the wall. They climbed it as fast as they could, and dropped over into the Wicked Prince's garden. The children were very glad to see them disappear, and Christiana began to thank the man for his kindness in coming to help them.

The First Trouble

"You need not thank me," he said; "but it is not well for you to travel alone. I was surprised that you did not ask Goodwill to send a guide with you. Your brothers are not yet old enough to be of much use."

Poor Matthew hung his head when he heard this, and felt ashamed of himself. He had intended to be so very brave, and he knew that he had acted like a coward.

"We never thought about the danger," said Christiana, "or that we should need a guide. I wish we *had* asked for one! Why did not Goodwill send someone with us, if he knew that it was not safe for us to be alone?"

"The King does not allow him to send guides unless the pilgrims wish for them," replied the man.

"Perhaps we had better turn back again," said Christiana, "and tell Goodwill that we are sorry."

"No, you must not turn back. I will take a message to him, and then when you come to the house of a man called Interpreter you can ask for a guide there."

"Oh," cried Mercy, when the man had left them, "I thought we should never have any trouble again!"

"*You* did not know," said Christiana; "but I did, and I ought to have realized that we do not only have to take care of *ourselves,* but my brothers and sister as well."

CHAPTER 7

The House of Interpreter

The children now went on their way very thoughtfully. Matthew ate no more fruit, and James and Joseph kept nearer Christiana than they had done in the morning. Presently Innocence began to grow sleepy, and Mercy said that her feet were aching. All the pilgrims felt very pleased when they saw a large house in the distance standing close to the wayside.

"That will be the house of Interpreter," said Christiana. "I must ask if we may sleep there, and do not let us forget to ask for a guide."

Now it happened that one of the King's servants, who had seen the children leaving the City of Destruction, had passed by the house of Interpreter a little earlier in the day. He had told his friends there of the new pilgrims who were on their way to the King's City. Interpreter's children remembered young Christian, and they knew that Christian had been very sorry because Christiana would not come with him when he began *his* journey.

"This must be the same Christiana," said one of them. "How pleased Christian will be when he meets her at the gates of the Heavenly City!"

The windows were wide open, and as the group of

pilgrims came up the pathway to the door of the house, they could hear Interpreter's children talking. Christiana fancied that she caught the sound of her own name. She knocked at the door, and a maid-servant came to open it.

"Who do you wish to see?" she asked.

"We were told that this house belongs to one of the King's servants," replied Christiana, "and that he allows pilgrims to rest here. Do you think we may stay until the morning? Why, little sister is tired, and we are afraid to go on traveling when it is dark."

Then the maid answered, "You must tell me your name and I will ask my master whether there is room for you in the house."

"My name is Christiana. I knew Christian, and I think he stayed here when he was a pilgrim. These are my three brothers, and this girl is our friend, Mercy."

The maid turned away, and went quickly to the room where Interpreter's children were sitting. "Can you guess who is at the door?" she cried. "Christiana herself, with her brothers, and her little sister, and a friend!"

The children were delighted, and ran at once to find their father, that they might tell him the good news. Interpreter was pleased also; and he hastened to the door, and welcomed the pilgrims.

"Are you really Christiana," he asked, "of whom Christian told us when he stayed here?"

"Yes," she replied; "and I wish now that I had come with him, for I have found that all the things he told

There were other pilgrims staying in the house.

me were true."

"You have done right to follow him," said Interpreter; "but we must not let you stand at the door. Come in, my children, and you shall rest."

There were other pilgrims staying in the house, and two or three of the King's servants, as well as Interpreter's own family. When the kind man led Christiana into the large hall where they were sitting, everyone seemed pleased to see her; and although Innocence was a little shy at first, and Mercy was silent among so many strangers, they soon felt happy and at home.

CHAPTER 8

The Man with the Straw

When the children had rested for a short time, Interpreter took them to see his picture of the Good Shepherd, and even Innocence understood how the lamb in the picture had been lost upon the mountains, and had been in great trouble until the Good Shepherd had found it, and taken it in His arms. They all stared at the picture, and were glad that the Shepherd was now their Prince.

After this, Interpreter brought his visitors into a darkened room, where a miserable-looking man was working busily. The floor of the room was covered with sticks, straw and mud, and the man held a rake in his hand, with which he was collecting all the rubbish into a heap. He did not look up when Interpreter opened the door, and he seemed to care for nothing but the straw and sticks he was raking from the mud.

"What is he collecting them for?" asked Matthew.

"He thinks they are very precious," replied Interpreter. "He has been serving the Wicked Prince for a long time, and he believes that some day, in the midst of this useless straw, he will find a wonderful treasure. The King is sorry for him, and every day He sends a messenger to offer him a golden crown instead of the straw."

"Will he *never* look up?" asked James.

The Man with the Straw

As Interpreter spoke, he pointed upwards; and when the children raised their heads, they saw above them, in the air, the figure of an angel, holding a bright crown.

"But he doesn't see it!" said Mercy.

"No," said Interpreter; "he will not look up."

Christiana shook her head sadly. "I am afraid I was just like him," she said. "I did not care about the King and His City; but I *do* care now!" Christiana smiled as she said this.

"Will he *never* look up?" asked James; and Joseph added, "How long will the angel wait for him?"

"I cannot tell you," replied Interpreter. "The King is very kind and very patient; but the man is so sure that he will find his treasure hidden in the rubbish, that I do not know whether he will *ever* look up!"

They went next into the garden, where the beds and borders were all filled with flowers. Interpreter told the children that the King's servants were like the flowers. Some plants were tall and stately, and no one could help seeing how beautiful they were; and others were quite tiny, and perhaps their blossoms were not even brightly colored, but had only a sweet scent. Still, the gardener loved *all* his flowers, and put each one in its best place in the garden.

"In the same way," said Interpreter, "the King loves all His servants, and gives them each a special place in His kingdom. Some have difficult and important work to do and others have only simple work, but not one of them is forgotten."

Christiana's Journey

It was now growing dark, for the sun had set, and presently the time came for supper. Interpreter kept the children near to him, and talked to them. He asked Christiana many questions about her old home, and even persuaded shy Mercy to tell him how she had seen the King's letter to Christiana. She explained she had suddenly made up her mind to be a pilgrim, even though she and her friends had laughed at first.

CHAPTER 9

Greatheart

In the morning the pilgrims were awakened by the light of the rising sun. They all got up quickly and dressed themselves, for they felt very eager to continue their journey.

But, when they came downstairs, Interpreter called them to him, and said, "These clothes that you are wearing will not do to travel in. We must give you some new ones out of the King's Treasury."

Christiana blushed. "I am so sorry," she said. "I washed and mended them as well as I could; but I know they are badly worn, and I could not make them new again."

"You did your best," replied Interpreter, kindly, "but even if they *were* new and clean, they would not be fit for you now. The King's pilgrims cannot wear garments that have been made in the cities of the Wicked Prince. Our good Prince has provided clothes for all His children, and the King will not receive you in any others." Then he handed Christiana a piece of paper rolled up. "You must look after this carefully," he said. "It is called your Roll of Faith. I have one for each of you. You will need to show them at the entrance to the Heavenly City. You must remember that you are now

37

all in the King's Family. You are His children for ever."

When Christian was traveling to the Heavenly City, the angels had met him at the Cross, and clothed him in the King's clothes. Christiana, Mercy, and the boys, and even Innocence, now received clothes which were just as spotless as Christian's; and when they looked at each other the children were almost frightened. If the journey was long and difficult, how could they possibly keep such clothes clean until they reached the gates of the City?

James and Joseph stood still, gazing down at themselves. "We can never play any more!" they said.

Interpreter smiled, and drew the boys nearer to him. "Do not be afraid," he said. "The King loves to see His children happy. Your clothes will not be harmed, unless you quarrel or play in a foolish way. You may run about as much as you like, as long as you do not leave the Way of the King."

Christiana and Mercy looked at each other when they heard this.

"The King is very good!" said Christiana; but Mercy did not speak. All this time she had been afraid, because she had entered the Gate to the King's Way without receiving a message from the King; but, now that she was clothed in garments from His own treasury, she felt that she was a true pilgrim, and she was ready to cry for joy.

When they were all prepared to leave the house, Interpreter called one of his young servants whose

He took the small girl from Christiana.

name was Greatheart, and said to him, "You must go with these children to the Palace Beautiful, and take care that none of the King's enemies come near, to hurt or frighten them on the way."

Greatheart was a tall, pleasant-looking boy, not much older than Christiana; but he wore a suit of bright armor, and he carried a sword at his side, so that the children felt sure he would be able to protect them if they met with any danger. Innocence stretched out her arms when she saw his brave but kind face; and he took the small girl from Christiana, saying, "Let me carry her, for she is tired."

Interpreter and his children came to the door and watched the young pilgrims set off: Greatheart carrying Innocence, while James and Joseph walked hand-in-hand beside him. Then came Christiana and Mercy, and, last of all, Matthew, whose head was aching, though he did not choose to say anything about it. The berries which he had eaten the day before were poisonous, and had done him no good; but he was ashamed to say how ill he felt, so he walked on behind Christiana, and hoped that the Palace Beautiful was not very far away.

He walked on behind Christiana.

CHAPTER 10

A Rest by the Cross

Before the day became hot, the pilgrims came to the Cross, and there Greatheart allowed them to rest. They all sat down upon the grass, and he told them how Christian's burden had fallen from his shoulders at this very place. Then Christiana began to question him about the Prince, and all that He had done for His servants. Greatheart loved the Prince, and was very willing to talk about Him, so the time slipped quickly away, and the children felt almost sorry when they had to leave their quiet resting place.

Not very far from the Cross they saw a sad sight. The year before, young Christian had tried to awaken three foolish boys who were lying on the grass by the wayside, with their feet bound in iron fetters. They did not listen to him, and he was obliged to leave them. But they never tried to undo their fetters, for they had no wish to continue their journey. All day long they sat idly by the road, doing everything they could to upset the King's pilgrims by talking to them, and trying to persuade them to leave the right path. At last they did so much mischief that the King would have patience with them no longer. He ordered them to be taken away. Their iron bands were hung where pilgrims passing by could see them, and take warning.

Innocence was too young to understand how evil the three boys had been; but the other children saw the fetters and asked why they were there.

Greatheart told them the whole sad story, and Christiana said, "I am glad they did not persuade Christian to leave the Way."

"So am I," said Mercy; "and I think it was very good thing that they were taken away. If they had been left, and we had been long here without Greatheart, they might have hurt or frightened us very much."

The road now brought the children to the foot of a steep hill called Hill Difficulty, and there Greatheart showed them two wrong paths which the Wicked Prince had made, one leading into the woods and the other into the dark mountains.

"Formalist and Hypocrisy were lost here," he said, "but Christian climbed the King's path up the hill. Since then, the King has sent men to put posts and chains across these wrong paths, so that His pilgrims may know they are not safe. But many pilgrims are so foolish that they take no notice of the chains, and try the paths, because they look so easy."

Just at the foot of the hill, and close to the King's Way, there was a spring of pure water. Greatheart pointed it out to the children, who were thirsty after walking in the sun. The water flowed into a deep pool, and in times past, this pool was as clear as crystal. But some of the Wicked Prince's servants, who were seeking for mischief to do, had found the spring, and they thought it would be a great thing to spoil it, and make it unfit for the King's pilgrims to drink from. So they trampled down the edges of the pool until the earth fell into the water, and made it too muddy for anyone to drink. They did this whenever they passed that way, and when Greatheart brought the pilgrims to the spring, he found it in a sad state.

But Christiana had packed a cup in the bag which the boys were carrying, and Greatheart told them to fill the cup with water, and let it stand for a few moments. Then the sand and soil sank to the bottom, and the water was left clear and bright; so they all drank and were much refreshed.

CHAPTER 11

Hill Difficulty

The path up the hillside was very hard to climb. Greatheart carried Innocence, and the children helped each other as much as they could; but the way was steep and rough, and the sun's rays were beating fiercely upon them as they toiled along.

Presently Mercy exclaimed, "What a dreadful hill! I don't think I can walk another step. May we not sit down and rest a little?"

When Joseph heard Mercy's words he, too, asked to stop, for although he had been doing his very best to climb the hill, he had fallen many times, and his hands and knees were bruised and sore.

"We will not stay here," said Greatheart. "We are very near to a shelter which the King has provided as a resting place for His pilgrims. Come here, Joseph, and take hold of my hand. You have climbed bravely, and we have now passed the worst part of the way."

Joseph felt happier when he heard Greatheart's words. Clasping his fingers tightly round those of his guide, he stepped out briskly, and in a few minutes the pleasant shelter came in sight, and the children hastened toward it.

"Oh!" cried Mercy, "it *is* good to rest when you are

tired! Our King is kind to make such a cool shady place for His pilgrims."

"You see," said Greatheart, "our Prince has traveled over this path Himself, so He knows how hard it is, and how much the pilgrims need a resting place." Then, calling James and Joseph to him, he asked them how they liked their pilgrimage.

"I didn't like it at all just now," said Joseph, "but I must thank you for helping me."

"*I* think," said James, "that I would rather be going *up* hill to the King's City, than *down* again toward the Wicked Prince's country!"

"Well said," agreed Greatheart, "and when you reach the King's City, you will be so happy that you will forget all the trouble you have had on your journey."

"Would you like something to eat while you are resting?" said Christiana. "Interpreter gave me some dried fruits and a piece of honeycomb."

She brought out the food and divided it among them, asking Greatheart to take his share; but the boy refused, saying he would soon be at home again, where plenty of food would be prepared for him; but they were pilgrims, and must make the most of what was provided for them.

CHAPTER 12

The King's Shelter

The pilgrims sat quietly in the King's shelter, eating their food and talking happily together, while Greatheart stood in the doorway, watching them.

"We must not rest too long," he warned them presently, "for we still have some distance to go, and the sun will soon be setting."

James and Joseph sprang up at once, and started off ahead of the others. All their bravery had come back again and they whispered to each other that they would not mind *very* much even if they *were* alone!

"Greatheart says the King is good, and we know He took care of Christian," said Joseph.

"Yes," said James, "and if we love Him, He will not let anyone hurt us; so I think we need not feel frightened any more."

When Christiana saw her two young brothers set off so quickly, she made haste to follow them. Interpreter had given her a bottle filled with refreshing drink, and she had not gone very far before she found that she had left this bottle in the King's shelter. James ran back to look for it, and while they were waiting for him Mercy said, "Did not Christian lose his Roll of Faith here? This seems to be a *forgetting* place!"

Greatheart smiled, and Christiana asked why pilgrims lost things in that shelter. "I remember," she said, "that I have heard of other pilgrims who have had to turn back here to look for something which they had left behind."

"It is only because they are careless," replied Greatheart. "They are tired with climbing the hill, and their rest makes them feel comfortable and happy. Very often they are tempted to sit longer than they ought to do, or they fall asleep. Then they start up in such a hurry that they are almost sure to lose something without noticing it."

James soon returned with the bottle in his hand, and the children made sure they each had their Roll of Faith. Then the pilgrims climbed steadily up the hill, until they reached the place where Mistrust and Timorous had met Christian, and frightened him by telling him of two lions. Those two boys were afterwards caught and punished by the King's servants, and a stone was placed by the wayside, with some words written upon it, advising pilgrims not to listen to persons who tried to persuade them that the Way of the King was too difficult or dangerous for them!

"But there *are* some lions, are there not?" asked Joseph.

"Yes," replied Greatheart; "but you need not be afraid of them."

Joseph looked at his brother. "I don't know whether I *should* like to meet a lion," he whispered. "It might be *very* savage. We will not be frightened, but we had

50

The two lions were wide awake.

better keep close to Greatheart!"

The sun had now set, and the shadows were deepening every moment. The two lions were wide awake when the children came in sight, and they both stood up and roared very loudly. Poor James and Joseph began to shake with fear, and they slipped behind Greatheart, who had drawn his sword, and held it in his hand ready to strike the lions if they sprang forward. The great beasts were chained, but the path between them was very narrow, and the savage creatures sometimes tried to seize pilgrims who wished to pass by them.

CHAPTER 13

Giant Grim and the Lions

Greatheart suddenly missed the two smallest boys, and looked round to see what had become of them.

"This is not right," he called to them. "You were running bravely on before us while there was no danger, and now you are hiding for fear of the lions! You must learn to trust in the King, and then you will not be so afraid."

But all the children were frightened, and even Christiana felt glad Greatheart was with them then; he looked so strong and unafraid.

"I don't know what we should have done," said Mercy, "if we had had no guide to go before us. Oh, do you see?" she added; "there is a terrible giant standing by the lions!"

The giant's name was Grim, and he had made a home for himself near to King's Way. He had taught the lions to obey him, and very often he came to feed them, and also to frighten any pilgrims who might be passing.

When Giant Grim saw Greatheart he stepped into the narrow path, and stood with his hands upon the necks of the two lions. Greatheart went boldly forward, but the children stood back, waiting to see what would happen.

"I shall not let you pass!"

Giant Grim and the Lions

"What business have you to walk upon this path?" roared the giant.

Greatheart answered, "I am taking these children home to the Heavenly City."

"This is not the way to the City!" said Grim. "I shall not let you pass. My lions are very fierce, and I can make them tear you in pieces!"

As Christiana looked before her she saw that the path was grown over with grass. The giant had frightened the King's pilgrims so much that for many weeks scarcely anyone had dared to pass that way. They had forgotten that the King would take care of them; but Christiana remembered what Wisdom had told her before she left home, and she suddenly cried out, "We may be children, but we are not afraid! Our King will take care of us, and will bring us safely past the lions!"

When the giant heard Christiana's voice, he laughed, and said that she should not go another step towards the King's City, for he and his lions could soon kill her and her companions!

Christiana held young Innocence very closely in her arms, and Mercy clung to her, scarcely daring to look up. James and Joseph were together. Even Matthew, who had never felt brave or happy since he had eaten the fruit from the Wicked Prince's garden, now wanted to be with the others. But Greatheart kept on his way, and the children crept after him.

His armor shone brightly before them in the shadows, for the daylight was nearly gone. In a moment his sword flashed through the air, and the giant moved back a few paces.

"Do you think you can *kill* me?" Grim shouted down at them.

"This path belongs to the King," said Greatheart. "Stand and defend yourself, for if you will not let these children pass, I will fight for them!"

CHAPTER 14

Watchful Receives the Children

When Greatheart raised his sword to strike the second time, the giant stooped down to unfasten the chains of the lions. But before he could do this the sharp weapon crashed through his helmet, and he fell upon his knees. He tried to get up, but the King helped His brave young soldier, and after a short struggle, the terrible giant lay dead at Greatheart's feet.

Then the lad turned round to look for the pilgrims. Mercy had hidden her face, but Christiana had watched the battle, though when the giant roared with pain, she could not help trembling. Greatheart held out his hand to her.

"Come," said he, "there is no danger now. Keep close to me, and the lions will not hurt you. Their master is dead, and they are too much frightened to spring at anyone."

The children saw that the lions were cowering upon the ground, so they hurried past them, and followed Greatheart to the gate of the Palace Beautiful. Watchful, the gatekeeper, looked out of his window, and asked who was there.

"It is I!" said Greatheart. Watchful knew his voice, and, taking his light, he came down quickly to the gate,

"How is it that you are so late?"

and opened it.

"How is it that you are so late?" he enquired.

"I have brought some pilgrims from the House of Interpreter," answered Greatheart. "We should have been here earlier, but the giant met us, and wished to turn us back again. I had to fight with him; but the King helped us, and I have killed him."

"I am glad that he is dead," said Watchful, "for he has given us much trouble. You must come in and rest yourself."

"No," replied Greatheart; "it is late, and my master will expect me to return tonight."

"Oh!" exclaimed Christiana. "How can we ever reach the Heavenly City unless you go with us?"

"Yes, indeed!" cried Mercy; "there are so many dangers, and we have no strength to fight with giants and wild beasts!"

Matthew and Joseph were afraid to speak, but James came close to Greatheart's side, and clasped his hand, saying, "Do, please, go all the way with us!"

"I will go with you very gladly," said Greatheart, "but I must first ask leave of my master. You should have spoken to him this morning when we were setting out. I must go back tonight, but I will tell him what you say, and perhaps he will let me come to you again."

So he bade them all good night, and was soon out of sight, for it was now completely dark

Then Watchful turned to Christiana, and asked her who she was, and where she had been living. Christiana told him, and he was pleased to hear that she was Christian's friend. Everyone in the Palace had liked the boy, and they had not forgotten how caringly he had spoken of Christiana.

Watchful rang his bell, and the maid who answered it went quickly back into the Palace with his message, and very soon a girl called Prudence came out with her sisters to welcome their new guests. Their mother, Discretion, had gone away to work for the King in another place, but her three daughters had the care of the Palace, and they received Christiana very kindly. The three daughters' names were Prudence, Piety and Charity.

CHAPTER 15

Mercy's Dream

"Supper is ready," said Prudence, as she led the children through the large hall; "so we will not tire you with talking tonight. You must sleep well, and tomorrow we want to hear all about your journey."

She looked so kind and she spoke so gently that Christiana took courage and said, "I don't know if I ought to ask for anything, but if you would let us sleep in the room where my friend Christian slept, we should be so very glad."

Prudence answered that no one was using the room, and she would be very pleased to let them have it; and there was also another room opening into it, which she said she would give to the boys.

Christiana and Mercy lay awake for a long time, talking of all that had happened since they left the City of Destruction. Innocence slept soundly in a small bed in the corner of the room.

"I didn't think," said Christiana, "when Christian used to tell me about the King, that I should ever be a pilgrim myself."

"No," said Mercy, "and you never thought you would come to stay in this grand palace and sleep in the very room Christian slept in."

"I had a lovely dream."

Mercy's Dream

Christiana sighed. "He was just like one of my own brothers, and I felt so sorry when they told me that he had gone away; but now I am happy again, for I know that he is with the King, and some day I shall meet him in the beautiful Heavenly City!"

"Listen!" cried Mercy; "is not that music? I am sure it is, and singing too. Did you ever hear anything so beautiful?"

The children lay still, while below, in the hall of the Palace, the King's servants sang His praises before they went to rest. When the music ceased, Christiana and Mercy whispered "Good night" to each other, and closed their eyes, feeling happier than they had ever done before.

In the morning Christiana said, "Do you know you were laughing in your sleep? Did you have a dream?"

Mercy's eyes shone as she answered, "I had a lovely dream! Did I really laugh?"

"Yes, you wakened me. What did you dream about?"

"I thought I was sitting in a lonely place, and crying because I felt miserable. A number of children came and teased me, and wanted to know what I was crying for. Some of them laughed at me and pushed me, so that I cried more than ever. At last I looked up and I saw an angel who came to me, and said, 'Mercy, what are you crying for?' I told him that I was very miserable. Then he spoke gently, and wiped the tears from my face, and he gave me a dress all shining with silver and gold. He put a crown upon my head, and took me by the hand, and we went on and on together until we came to a great golden gate. The angel knocked, and the gate was opened, and he took me in, and brought me to a throne where the King was sitting. Oh, Christiana, He looked *so* kind and gracious! I didn't feel the least bit frightened, and the King held out His hand to me, saying 'Welcome, my daughter!' Everything was bright, just like stars in the night, and I thought I saw Christian, and then I woke. Are you sure I laughed?"

"Yes, and I don't wonder, when you had such a dream! I think it must be time for us to get up now, and we had better waken the boys!"

CHAPTER 16

Pleasant Days

"Your friend Christian stayed here more than one night," said Mercy, while they were dressing. "If Prudence invites us to stay, what shall you say? She looks so pleasant; I should like to make friends with her and with her sisters."

"We will see what they wish us to do," replied Christiana. "Perhaps all the pilgrims are allowed to stay here for a few days."

After breakfast, Prudence, Piety and Charity began to talk to their new guests, and presently Prudence said, "We should like you to stay with us for a while, if you think you can be happy here."

"Oh, yes!" answered Christiana. "We should enjoy it very much indeed."

The pilgrims spent a whole month at the Palace Beautiful, and during that time many things happened. Prudence and her sisters were all very kind, and sometimes Prudence called the three boys together, and questioned them to see what they knew. Christiana had tried to teach them about the King and His Son, and she was pleased to hear that they answered well.

"You must take pains to remember what your older sister teaches you," said Prudence; "and when you hear

Christiana's Journey

people talking of the King, it will be right for you to listen, that you may learn more about Him and His Son. You are all so fond of reading," she continued, "and that is a good thing, but you may be sure that you will never find any better book than the King's own Book, the one which Christian loved so dearly. There are stories in it for children, and wise sayings, and the more you read in it, the more you will love it, for it will teach you how to serve the King faithfully."

Not far from the Palace lived a boy whose name was Brisk. He was bright and good-natured. Prudence and her sisters hoped that he would one day be a true servant of the King. He often came to the Palace and talked to them, but Prudence had never yet been able to persuade him to give up his careless ways and become a pilgrim. He always said he was too busy, but that some day he would find time to begin his journey.

When the young pilgrims had been at the Palace for about a week, Brisk came in one morning. Mercy had a very attractive face, and when Brisk began to talk to her, he thought she was the nicest girl he had ever seen. He asked her to come with him to see his brothers and sisters: but Mercy answered that she had a great deal of work to do, for she did not think that Prudence would be pleased if she left the Palace.

Brisk came to the Palace nearly every day that he might talk to Mercy. She had asked Prudence about him, and she told her that he had not yet learned to love the King, although he liked to come to the Palace and to talk with the pilgrims.

66

Pleasant Days

"He is a pleasant boy," thought Mercy, "but he will not be a good friend for me if he does not love the King." So, whenever he came, she sat quietly sewing, and did not take much notice of him. Prudence, Piety and young Charity were always busy, too.

CHAPTER 17

Matthew's Illness

Brisk was upset when he found that Mercy did not care to talk to him, and one day he said to her, "You are *always* sewing!"

Mercy looked up smiling. "Yes," she said; "if I have no work for myself, there is always plenty to do for other people."

"You must earn a lot of money!" said Brisk.

"I don't do it for money," replied Mercy.

"What *do* you do it for, then?"

"I am making some clothes for Charity. She gives them away to people who are very poor."

"Oh!" said Brisk, and he looked so surprised that Mercy could not help smiling.

He did not come to the Palace again for some days, and when Prudence asked him why he had forsaken his friend, he replied that Mercy was very pretty, but she had such foolish ways!

However, Mercy was not sorry that he did not come. "I could not work so well when he was talking to me," she said; "and I don't wish for any friends who do not serve the King."

"That is right," said Prudence, "you cannot help meeting boys and girls who are like Brisk, but it is wise not to let them take you away from the Way of the King."

Christiana was now very worried indeed. Matthew had been feeling ill all this time, and each day at the Palace when he got up his head seemed to ache more, and he often felt so sick and faint that he could scarcely stand. At last he was obliged to tell his sister, and Christiana wondered what could have made him ill, for she had forgotten all about the fruit which he had eaten.

The next morning he could not lift his head from his pillow when Christiana came to waken him, and she made haste to finish dressing that she might ask Prudence what she must do. Prudence sent at once for a doctor, an old man named Skill. He was not long in coming, and Christiana took him up to see the sick boy. Matthew lay in bed, and Joseph sat near to him, for the brothers were very fond of each other.

"What has he been eating?" asked Skill.

"Nothing but wholesome food," said Christiana.

Skill shook his head. "He has been eating poison, and if the medicine I can give him will not take effect, he will die."

Poor Christiana was so troubled that she could not speak, but Joseph exclaimed, "Oh, don't you remember the berries? They hung over the wall by the Gate to the King's Way, and Matthew ate some, but you made *us* throw them away."

"Yes, he did," replied Christiana; "I told him not to take them, but I remember he would not listen to me."

Matthew's Illness

"Ah!" said the doctor, "I was sure he had eaten something poisonous! And that fruit is worse than any other, for it grows in the Wicked Prince's own garden!"

The tears ran down Christiana's cheeks, for Matthew lay upon the bed looking so white and still that she feared the doctor's words would come true, and that he would really die.

"What shall I do for him?" she cried. "Oh, how could I let him eat those berries!"

When Skill saw how frightened she was, he spoke very gently. "Do not be too unhappy. I have one of the King's medicines with me, and if he has not eaten a great quantity of the fruit, it may do him good."

CHAPTER 18

The Golden Anchor

The medicine which Skill prepared tasted very sweet, but Matthew was too ill to care what anyone said to him. For a long time neither the doctor nor Christiana could persuade him to take it; but at last, after a great deal of trouble, he was made to drink some. At first Matthew complained that it tasted bitter, but soon he found the taste sweet.

Although for many hours he was still in pain, toward evening Matthew began to grow easier, and Christiana was thankful to see him fall into a quiet sleep.

The next day he was able to get up for a little while, but his illness had made him so weak that he could not walk without the help of a stick. Everyone was very kind to him, and Christiana's heart was full of thankfulness to the King for sparing his life.

"I should like to have some of that medicine always with me," she said; and Skill was very willing to prepare some for her, and told her how and when it should be used.

It was perhaps a good thing for Matthew that he had suffered so much, for he was now more ready to listen to his sister's advice; and, instead of thinking that he

He was now more ready to listen.

The Golden Anchor

was too old to be taught by Prudence, he came to her as James and Joseph did, and asked her about many things which he did not understand.

The time passed pleasantly away, and toward the end of the month Joseph reminded Christiana that she had wanted Greatheart to guide them to the Heavenly City.

"He was so good to us, and he is so brave," said her young brother. "How can we find out if Interpreter will let him come?"

"I think I must write to him," said Christiana. So she wrote a letter that very day, and gave it to Watchful, who sent a messenger with it to the House of Interpreter. In the evening the messenger returned, saying that Interpreter had read the letter, and he was sending Greatheart to guide the pilgrims on their journey.

Prudence and her sisters were sorry to part with the young pilgrim, and in those last days they took care to show them all the treasures for which the Palace Beautiful was so famous. Among other things, Christiana saw and admired a miniature golden anchor.

"You shall have it for yourself, if you like," said Piety; "you can wear it as a brooch, and when you look at it, do not forget what it means."

"What *does* it mean?" asked Mercy.

"You know what is the use of an anchor? If it is firmly fixed, the sailors do not mind how rough the sea may be. The anchor holds their vessel safely, though the waves may be tossing and the wind roaring all around them. So if you love the King, trust that He will help you and will keep your heart from failing; and, though you may be in the greatest danger or difficulty, you will never be really afraid."

The anchor hung upon a slender chain, and Christiana clasped it round her neck, saying, "I am so glad to have it, for it will help us all to remember what you have taught us."

While they were talking, a knock was heard at the gate, and soon Watchful rang his bell, and sent word that Greatheart had arrived. Young Innocence ran at once into his arms, and, as he lifted her up, James and Joseph stood by him on either side.

"I have brought a gift for you from my master," said Greatheart, when he was able to speak to Christiana. He showed her a large store of dried fruit from Interpreter. "It can be easily carried, and you will find it useful when we are at a distance from any houses."

CHAPTER 19

The Valley of Humiliation

Christiana was very pleased at Interpreter's kindness, and she had also to thank Prudence for making their stay at the Palace Beautiful so pleasant.

It was early when Greatheart arrived, and the children were not long in preparing for their journey.

"We will go to the bottom of the hill with you," said Prudence. "The path is slippery and rather dangerous."

As they passed through the gate, Christiana said goodby to Watchful, and asked him whether any other pilgrims had gone by that day. Watchful said, "No"; but told them that a man had rested in his lodge the night before, and had told him of some pilgrims who had been attacked and robbed by the Wicked Prince's servants.

"But you need not be troubled," he said; "for our King's soldiers heard of it, and they pursued the robbers, and they are now in prison."

Christiana and Mercy had turned pale when Watchful mentioned the robbers; but Matthew touched his sister's hand, whispering, "You need not be afraid, Christiana. You are forgetting that we have Greatheart with us."

So the party set out, and began to descend the steep path which led into the Valley of Humiliation. It was

"He knows his Master is pleased with him."

very slippery, but Piety carried Innocence, while Greatheart went first with Christiana, and Matthew came behind them all with Mercy, James and Joseph.

At last they reached the valley in safety, and Piety said, "It was in this valley that Christian fought his battle with Apollyon, but if he comes out to meet you, you must not be frightened. Greatheart will take good care of you, and the King will be ready to help you."

Then the three sisters returned to the Palace, and the children followed their guide across the valley. It was a very lovely spot, and at this time the ground was covered with lilies, which filled the air with their sweet scent.

"I should not have thought that the Wicked Prince or his servants would ever come here," said Christiana. "It is so very peaceful!"

"It is *our* Prince's favorite valley," replied Greatheart. "He once lived here for a long time. But you must not expect to be able to find any place where the Wicked Prince and his servants do not come, until you are in the King's own country."

Presently Innocence pointed to some sheep feeding, with lambs frisking happily beside their mothers. A boy was taking care of them, but he was among the trees, where he could not see the pilgrims, although they could see him. He was singing to himself.

"He is poor," said Greatheart, "yet he is happy. He works faithfully, and knows that his Master is pleased with him. The King has given him these few sheep to care for, and he looks for nothing more than to work for his Master."

Christiana's Journey

The young pilgrims were now drawing near to the entrance of the Dark Valley. Christian had to pass through that terrible place in the night. It was now early in the afternoon, and Greatheart hoped that he would be able to guide the children safely over the worst part before the darkness fell upon them.

It was always very gloomy in the Dark Valley, for the rocks were high, and leaned toward each other, so that the sun could never shine upon the path below. Greatheart looked at the children as they drew closer to him. Mercy held Christiana's hand, and her lips were trembling, but Christiana pointed to the anchor which she wore, so, though their faces were pale, Greatheart knew that they were both thinking of the King, and that they would follow Him bravely through the terrors of the valley.

James and Joseph were in great fear. The strange noises among the rocks, and the dimness of the light, frightened them more than the sight of the narrow, dangerous pathway. Matthew told his brothers to walk before him, and did his best to cheer and encourage them.

"Follow me carefully," said Greatheart, "and do not tremble, or you will miss your footing. Remember that if you trust in the King, the Wicked Prince and his servants cannot harm you."

But poor James had not gone very far before his feet suddenly slipped, and he would have fallen if Matthew had not caught him with his hands. Greatheart stepped back, and stooping down, lifted the boy upon his knee.

The Valley of Humiliation

Christiana looked anxiously into his face, for she feared that someone had hurt him.

"He is only tired," said Greatheart. "If you will give him a little of Skill's medicine, he will soon revive."

Christiana persuaded the boy to take it, and presently he opened his eyes and began to feel better.

"I was frightened," he said. "I thought I saw horrible things. Will the King be angry?"

"No," replied Greatheart. "He knows how terrible this valley is, and that you are only a boy."

CHAPTER 20

The Dark Valley

"Where did Apollyon meet Christian?" asked James. "Shall we see the place?"

"We shall come to it presently," replied Greatheart. "Apollyon is the King's enemy, and he often meets pilgrims in that part of the valley. It is called Forgetful Green."

"Why?" asked Mercy.

"Because when pilgrims have been staying at the Palace Beautiful, and are walking along this pleasant path, they often forget that the Way of the King is not *all* smooth and easy, and they begin to think that all dangers are past."

"Did Christian forget?"

"I think he did, but you know he loved the King, and he would not let Apollyon persuade him to give up his journey."

It was not long before they reached the place where the battle was fought, and Greatheart told the story over again. The boys loved to hear of Christian's bravery, and how the King had helped him to overcome his enemy. Greatheart also showed them the rock by which the wounded pilgrim had rested after the battle, and he told them of the dream which had comforted Christian so much.

CHAPTER 21

Terrors of the Way

The Dark Valley was indeed a terrible place, and even Christiana grew timid, and fancied that she could see strange shapes among the shadows. But Greatheart went steadily forward, and the pilgrims followed him closely until they had passed half way through the valley.

Then Mercy, turning to look behind her, saw a lion coming after them. It began to roar as it drew near, and Greatheart made the children go before him, while he waited for the savage beast. When the creature saw that its enemy was prepared to fight instead of running away, it crouched down upon the path, and came no further.

Soon after this Greatheart himself had to stop, for he found that the narrow path had been broken away, and a deep pit lay just before him. He did not know how to take the pilgrims over it, for although a tall active lad like Matthew might have been able to cross it, the girls and the younger boys could not possibly have done so. And, all in a moment, while he was considering what to do, a thick mist rose up around them, so that they could not even see each other.

"This is dreadful!" cried Christiana. "What can we do?"

Christiana's Journey

"We can only pray to the King," answered Greatheart; "He will not leave us. He is here, although we cannot see Him. Perhaps the pit is not a real one. The Wicked Prince has power in this valley to make us think that we can see dangers when they are not really there. We must stand still until the mist clears away."

The children obeyed, keeping hold of each other's hands, and praying in their hearts to the King to deliver them.

"It must have been worse for poor Christian than it is for us," said Christiana presently. "He was alone, and he came through the valley in the *night!*"

"The King was watching over him," said Greatheart. "I have brought many pilgrims along this pathway, and sometimes the danger has been far greater than it is now, but the King has always helped us, and we have been brought out safely."

Greatheart's words comforted the pilgrims, and they waited patiently, although the strange noises and the sound of footsteps hurrying up and down were very terrifying in the darkness. But no one came near to hurt them; and after a time a light began to break through the mist, and soon it was clear enough to see the ground.

"It is as I thought," said Greatheart; "the pit was not real. See, the pathway is quite firm."

The children were thankful, and gladly went on their way. But a new trouble soon came upon them. The valley was now filled with a poisonous vapor, so that the air was scarcely fit to breathe.

"This is not a nice part of our pilgrimage," sighed Mercy. "I do not like it so well as I did at the Gate, or with Interpreter, or at the Palace Beautiful."

"Ah," said Matthew, "but think how much worse it would be to live *here* always, as we might have to do if we served the Wicked Prince! Perhaps the King wishes us to pass through this dreadful place so that we may learn to care more about being with Him in the Heavenly City."

"That is just the reason," said Greatheart.

"Shall we soon be able to see the end of the valley?" asked Joseph, for he was beginning to feel very tired with walking upon the narrow path.

"We are almost through," answered Greatheart, "but now you must be very careful, for we are coming to the snares!"

CHAPTER 22

The End of the Valley

When Christian had passed this way, he had been very troubled by finding the ground near the end of the Dark Valley covered with snares placed cunningly up and down to entrap the pilgrims. Greatheart now led his friends slowly along, but they found it very difficult to walk upon this dangerous path without falling or getting their feet entangled. Presently they saw a man lying by the wayside.

"His name is Heedless," said Greatheart, "and he fancied he could walk safely here without the help of the King. But as he hurried carelessly along, his feet were caught in a snare which threw him down. His companion, who was called Take-heed, could not unfasten it."

"Did Take-heed escape?" asked Mercy.

"Yes, but it made him very sad to leave his friend in the power of the Wicked Prince."

Just at the end of the valley Christian had passed by the cave of the two old giants. A young giant had now come to live in their cave. His name was Maul. He knew Greatheart, and hated him very much, and always tried to hinder him when he brought the King's pilgrims out of the valley.

He rushed suddenly at the boy.

The End of the Valley

As Greatheart drew near to the cave, Maul looked out, and, seeing the pilgrims, he cried, "How often have you been forbidden to do this?"

"To do what?" asked Greatheart.

"You know what I mean," answered the giant angrily; "but I will put a stop to it." And, seizing his great club, he came down the rocky path toward the King's Way.

"We will not fight," said Greatheart quietly, "until you tell me why you are attacking me."

"Because you are a robber," said the giant. "You carry off children from the cities of my Prince, and take them into a strange country, and no one knows what will become of them!"

"I am a servant of the *King*," said Greatheart. "I am not a robber. My Master has commanded me to bring the children safely home to Him, and if you wish to fight me because I obey Him, I am quite ready!"

When the giant heard this, he rushed suddenly upon the boy, and struck him such a terrible blow with his club that Greatheart fell upon his knees. The young pilgrims gave a scream of fright, for they thought that their faithful guide would be killed; but Greatheart quickly sprang up again, and wounded the giant's arm with his sword. After this they had a long struggle, while the children watched and trembled, for although they knew that Greatheart was brave and trusted in the King to help him, they could see that the giant was very strong, and they feared he might gain the victory.

At last the giant became tired, and would fight no

longer, but he still refused to let Greatheart pass. He sat down by the wayside to rest, and Greatheart turned away and prayed to the King to give him new strength so that he might win the battle.

The pilgrims prayed also. Giant Maul saw what they were doing, and it made him feel afraid, for he knew that the King heard the prayers of His servants, and that children had sometimes been able, by His help, to overcome the strongest giants. However, he determined to fight more fiercely than before. He hoped that he would be able to kill Greatheart; for if he could seize the pilgrims and carry them back into the country of the Wicked Prince, he would receive a great reward.

CHAPTER 23

Greatheart Overcomes the Giant

The King did not forsake Greatheart. When the fight began again, the lad felt that his strength and courage were increasing every moment, and before long he succeeded in bringing the giant to the ground. Maul cried for mercy, and Greatheart allowed him to rise; but as he got up the giant struck at the young soldier with his club. The blow fell upon Greatheart's head, and if his helmet had been less strong it might have killed him. After that Maul's courage failed. Greatheart's sword had wounded him in his side, and he began to feel faint, and could no longer hold his heavy club. It fell from his hands, and that ended the battle. In a few moments Greatheart was standing alone upon the pathway, and the giant lay dead at his feet.

The children were full of joy, for although the fight had been terrible to see, they knew that the giant was one of the King's enemies, and that it was right for Greatheart to kill him. Near to the cave in which he had lived there were a number of large stones. The boys climbed up the rocks, and rolled several of the stones down to the pathway, and built them up into a pillar, upon which they placed the head of the giant, so that pilgrims who came out of the Dark Valley might see it, and know that their enemy was dead.

At a little distance from the cave there was a green mound overlooking the plain. When the children came to it, Greatheart advised them to sit down and rest, and eat some of the fruit which he had brought from the House of Interpreter. As they sat comfortably upon the grass, Christiana asked him whether he had been wounded.

"Not much," he replied; "my armor is so good. I have only a few cuts and bruises, which will soon be healed."

"Were you not frightened when the giant struck you with his club?" said Christiana.

Greatheart smiled. "Yes; but I knew the King would help me. The Prince Himself has often been wounded, but He has always conquered in the end, and He will not let His servants be overthrown if they are faithful to Him."

It was now late in the evening, and although it was summertime, the light was beginning to fade, so the pilgrims were obliged to hasten on their journey. Many fine oak trees grew upon the plain, and some of them stood quite close to the King's Way.

As the children walked quickly along they saw an old man sitting upon the ground under one of the trees. His staff was in his hand, but his eyes were closed, and he seemed to be asleep.

"He is dressed like a pilgrim," said Matthew.

"Yes," said Greatheart, "he is a pilgrim; and we

must not leave him sleeping here."

He touched the man's shoulder to waken him, and the poor old pilgrim sprang up trembling, for he thought the enemy was trying to seize him.

"What is it?" he cried. "Who are you?"

CHAPTER 24

Honesty

Greatheart was sorry that he had startled the man. "You need not be afraid of us," said he, "we are all friends."

But the old pilgrim was not satisfied. He looked anxiously at Greatheart and Matthew, and asked again who they were.

"My name is Greatheart," said the lad; "and I am taking these children to the Heavenly City."

Then the man smiled, for he had heard of Greatheart before. "I was afraid that you were robbers!" he said; "but I see now that you are the King's servants."

"What would you have done if we *had* been robbers?" asked Greatheart, for the stranger did not look fit to defend himself.

"I know I am only a feeble old man," he replied; "but I would have called to the King and fought. Yes, I would have fought as long as I had any breath, and I do not think even you two strong lads would have overcome me!"

"You speak like a good pilgrim," said Greatheart. "Will you not tell us your name?"

The old man shook his head. "Oh, never mind my name! I am only a poor fellow, and I used to live in a

97

"I was afraid that you were robbers!"

little place called Stupidity, about four leagues from the City of Destruction."

"Oh, is it *you*. Honesty," cried Greatheart, seizing his hand.

"Well, yes," he replied, "my name is Honesty, but it is only by the help of the King that I can be true to it. How did you know anything about me?"

"I have heard the Prince speaking well of you," said Greatheart, and then the old pilgrim's face flushed all over with pleasure, for he loved the Prince with his whole heart.

Honesty soon made friends with the young pilgrims. They were pleased with his kind, good-natured face, and Christiana and Mercy thought that his white hair made him look handsome. As for Innocence, she was not quite ready to let him take her in his arms, but she stood close.

As they went along in the twilight, Greatheart talked to Honesty, of his pilgrimage, and presently asked him if he remembered one of his old friends named Fearing.

"Yes, indeed," said the old man; "I have often thought of him since the time when we lived near to each other. Has he reached the City safely?"

"My Master sent me with him from our house," replied Greatheart. "He was always afraid, for although he loved the King, he thought that he would be turned away from the gates of the Heavenly City. He fancied that he was too weak and poor for the King to notice him, and that he would not be helped as other pilgrims are. We were told that he stayed upon the plain for many days

near to the Slough of Despair, because he felt sure that
he would sink in it. Many people offered to lead him
over it, but he only wept; and though he watched them
cross in safety, he would not venture."

"But he *did* cross," said Mercy.

"Oh, yes, after a long time! One bright morning he
took courage, and when he reached the firm ground
beyond the Slough, he could scarcely believe that the
danger was really past. Then, at the Gate to the King's
Way, he behaved in the same way. He did not think he
would be received, so he would not knock. Other
pilgrims came to the gate, and Goodwill let them in,
but Fearing drew back, so that the gatekeeper never
saw him. At last he crept up to the Gate, and gave one
timid knock. Goodwill came at once, and seeing no one,
he stepped out upon the plain. Poor Fearing lay
trembling on the ground, but Goodwill lifted him up,
and spoke kindly to him."

"I am sure he would!" said Mercy; for she remembered
how she had been almost as timid herself before she
entered the Way of the King.

"Goodwill is a kind friend to everyone," said Honesty.
"But tell me what happened to Fearing. I know very
well what a strange man he was."

CHAPTER 25

Fearing's Pilgrimage

The rest of Fearing's story was soon told. Greatheart said Goodwill had written a letter to Interpreter, asking him to send a guide to go with the poor man from his house all the way to the Heavenly City. But Fearing spent several days and nights outside Interpreter's gates before anyone knew that he was there. Then, one morning, Greatheart happened to see him from one of the windows and went down to speak to him. He was cold and weak for want of food, but he brought out Goodwill's letter, and after a little trouble Greatheart persuaded him to enter the house.

"And you were with him always from that time?" asked Honesty.

"Yes. He was pleased when we came to the Cross, and he did not mind the Hill Difficulty, or the lions. He was not afraid of such things. He only feared lest the King should not think him fit to be a pilgrim. At the Palace Beautiful he was very happy. He would not have much to do with the family, or with their other guests, but he liked to hear them talk. There is a large curtain in the hall, and he used to sit behind it, where he could not be seen, and listen to what was said. We stayed a long time in the Valley of Humiliation, for my Master told me not to hurry him, and he seemed to love the grass and flowers so much that he could not bear to leave them."

"How did he pass through the Dark Valley?"

"I was afraid it would be very terrible to him, and indeed it was; but the King did not allow him to be troubled as many pilgrims are. I never saw the valley so light or so quiet at any other time. In Vanity Fair he was very angry at the wickedness he saw around him. He was braver there than anywhere, and was ready to fight the enemies of the King at every turn. However, we passed through the town without being hurt, and after traveling slowly for several weeks we came to the River."

"Was he not satisfied when he saw the gates of the Heavenly City?"

"Not at first. He wandered along the shore, looking across at the bright walls, and saying that he was sure he would never be received there. He said that he would be lost in the River. But when the message came for him, I went down to watch him crossing, and the water was so low that he went over quite easily. Then the angels met him, and I saw him no more."

Honesty seemed very glad to hear of his old friend's pilgrimage, and that he had reached the City safely. When Greatheart had finished his story, Christiana said, "I thought perhaps *other* pilgrims were never afraid that the King would not receive them. But I have felt afraid so often."

"So have I," said Mercy.

"I have too," said Matthew; "and I wondered whether the King would be displeased with me for it."

"No," replied Greatheart, "He will not be displeased. I think all good pilgrims feel anxious sometimes."

"If they were quite satisfied with themselves," said Honesty, "it would show that they were not the King's true servants. No true pilgrim can reach the Heavenly City by trying to be good enough. The King will only let us in because of His Son. I once traveled a little way with a pilgrim whose name was Self-will. He never troubled himself at all about loving the King. He thought he need only try to follow this path until he came to the City, and he would *surely* be received there, but he was wrong.

While Honesty was talking about this foolish pilgrim, a man passed by who said to Greatheart, "You must be careful, for there are some robbers out tonight upon this plain."

Greatheart was glad of the warning, and both he and Matthew kept watch as they went along; but they did not meet the robbers, who had perhaps heard of Greatheart, and would not dare to attack him.

CHAPTER 26

The House of Gaius

Innocence was now sound asleep in Christiana's arms, with her head on her sister's shoulder. The two youngest boys were beginning to feel tired and cross after their long day. The sun had set, and the stars were shining overhead, but Christiana did not like the thought of sleeping out of doors. She asked Greatheart whether he knew of a house where they could rest.

"There is a friend of mine," said Honesty, "a man named Gaius, who lives on the Way of the King. We shall soon be in sight of his house, and I am sure he will let us stay the night."

Gaius received the pilgrims very kindly. He always kept several rooms ready for the use of travelers, and his servants were as pleased as their master to have the opportunity to shelter the King's pilgrims. While the cook was preparing supper, Gaius brought his guests into his own parlor, where they were very glad to sit down and rest. He had much to say to his old friend Honesty, and also to Greatheart, and the children listened quietly, and felt very happy.

Presently a maid came in and spread a cloth upon the table, and laid out the plates and bread. Then the cook sent up the supper, and the hungry travelers were thankful to see the good food placed before them—meat and potatoes, milk and butter and honey, and a dish of large red apples and other fruit.

When Matthew saw the fruit, he blushed, for he thought of the poisoned berries which had made him so ill when he was at the Palace Beautiful.

"May we eat them?" he asked.

"Oh, yes!" replied Gaius, "they are wholesome fruit." Then Matthew told him why he was afraid.

"But those were *poisoned* berries," said Gaius. *"This* fruit is from the King's orchards, and will hurt no one."

After supper Gaius gave the boys some nuts to crack, and while they ate them he went on talking to Greatheart. At last Christiana thought it would be better for the younger ones to go to bed, and she was also very tired herself. So Gaius showed her the rooms which had been made ready, one for her, Innocence and Mercy, and one for the boys. Before long they were all asleep in their comfortable beds. As for Honesty, he was so pleased to see his old friend, Gaius, again, that he would sit by the fire all night to talk to him, and Greatheart sat with him, until the sun rose, and the servants began to put the house in order for the day.

While they were at breakfast, Gaius told his guests of a wicked giant named Slay-good, who had come to live among the hills about a mile from his house.

"He is very strong and fierce," said Gaius, "but if you will go with me to attack him, I am sure the King will help us, and give us strength to destroy him."

So Christiana, Mercy and the other children were

left to spend the morning in the house, while Gaius took Greatheart and Matthew to look for the giant. Honesty said he would go with them, for although he was old, he was very brave, and said he liked to see the King's enemies defeated.

Now it happened that, the day before, the giant had seized a poor pilgrim named Feeble-mind, and when Gaius and his party appeared, he was just preparing to kill him. But he was forced to come out of his cave and defend himself when the King's servants began to attack him. Feeble-mind lay still in the darkness, and when he heard the sound of voices he rejoiced, for he felt sure that the King had sent someone to save his life.

The battle lasted for an hour, but Giant Slay-good was overcome at last, and Gaius searched the cave carefully to see whether any captives were hidden there. Feeble-mind was soon found, and carried back to the house, and when he had eaten some food and rested a little, he was able to tell his story.

CHAPTER 27

Feeble-Mind and Ready-to-Halt

Feeble-mind had never been strong, and he seemed scarcely fit to take a long journey.

"But," he said, "I have made up my mind that I will find the King's City, and if I am too weak to walk all the way, I will crawl on my hands and knees! Everyone has been very good to me, and I have come thus far in safety. I could not have climbed the Hill Difficulty, but Interpreter sent a servant with me, and he carried me on his back to the top of the rocky path. This is the worst thing that has happened to me, but as I lay in the giant's cave last night, I prayed to the King, and I felt sure He would save me. And you see He *has* saved me!"

The pilgrims were glad to have been able to rescue Feeble-mind, and they all talked till late into the night.

Gaius had a young daughter, whose name was Phoebe. She now wished very much to go to the Heavenly City, and her father thought that it would be good for her to travel with Christiana and Mercy. So they stayed a few days, while she prepared for her journey. On the last day Gaius made a feast for them, and when it was over Greatheart asked what he must pay for their lodging. But Gaius would not take any money. He said he loved the King, and for His sake he

"I will find the King's city!"

Feeble-Mind and Ready-to-Halt

kept his house open for any pilgrims who chose to stay there.

When the children were saying goodby, Greatheart saw Feeble-mind standing silently in the doorway, and he said to him, "Are you not coming with us? The King will be glad for us to help you on your way."

Feeble-mind shook his head. "I am afraid I should delay you," he replied. "You are all strong and active, and I am so weak! Then I am not merry as these children are, and I should make them feel sad with my dull ways."

"Oh, no, you will not!" cried Christiana. "Do come with us, and we will cheer and help you."

"Yes," said Greatheart, "it is not wise for you to travel alone. We shall be sorry if we have to leave you behind."

The tears came into the poor lad's eyes; but he could not make up his mind to go with Greatheart, for he was really afraid of hindering the pilgrims by his weakness. However, while they were all standing together on the pathway, they heard the sound of footsteps approaching, and another pilgrim came in sight. His name was Ready-to-halt. He was young, but he was so lame that he had to walk with crutches. When Feeble-mind saw him, he exclaimed, "Oh! how did you come here?" for he had known him before.

The lad smiled as he held out his hand. "And how did *you* come up here?" he asked. "I think we are both bound for the same place."

"You are lame, and I am weak," replied Feeble-mind,

"but the King will not turn us away from the gates of His City. I was just wishing for a companion, and no one could suit me better than you."

"I shall be only too glad to go with you," said Ready-to-halt.

Then Greatheart and Honesty spoke to him, and soon everything was settled.

"We cannot travel very fast," said Greatheart, "but if you are not able to keep up with us, we can always wait for you."

So the pilgrims set off once more. Honesty walked first with Greatheart, and Matthew and his two young brothers followed him. Then came Christiana, Mercy and Phoebe, little Innocence, and last of all, the lame boy and Feeble-mind.

"I am sure we shall be able to help each other," said Ready-to-halt, "and when you are tired I will lend you one of my crutches."

CHAPTER 28

Crossing the Plain

The pilgrims spent the day in crossing the plain. After walking for several hours they saw the walls and gates of Vanity Fair in the distance before them. The great towers rose darkly against the clear sky, and Christiana began to feel afraid as she drew near to the city of the Wicked Prince.

"It is such a dreadful place!" she said.

"Did not poor Faithful die there?" asked Mercy.

"Yes," answered Phoebe. "The people treated him very cruelly, and they kept Christian in prison for some time."

"Do you think that *we* shall be put in prison?" asked Mercy.

Christiana's face grew white, and she held Innocence more closely. "If we are separated from each other," she said, "do not let us forget all that has happened while we have been together. The King has been very good to us, and we know that He is always watching over us. If we have to suffer, we must be brave because we love Him."

Feeble-mind and Ready-to-halt were walking just behind the girls, and could hear all they said.

"Are you afraid?" asked Feeble-mind.

"I think we all are," replied Christiana.

"Do we *have* to pass through the city?" said Mercy. "Is there no other way?"

Ready-to-halt looked kindly at the frightened girl. "We could go *round,*" he said, "but then we might not find our way into the right path again!"

"I think we must go straight on," said Phoebe. "I have heard my father, Gaius, say that the people are less rough than they used to be. Their Wicked Prince has told them to make things seem pleasant in the city, so that pilgrims may feel inclined to give up their journey and stay for ever."

Greatheart and Honesty turned round at this moment, and waited for the rest of the party to catch up with them.

"We shall have to spend the night in Vanity Fair," said Greatheart; "for if we pass straight through the city, we shall not be able to reach another safe resting place before the darkness comes on."

"Where can we sleep?" asked Christiana. "Will not the people ill-treat us?"

"I think not," replied Greatheart. "I have brought many pilgrims safely through the city, and I know an old man who will give us a lodging, and be very pleased to see us."

"Does he love the King?" asked Mercy.

"Yes. The King has commanded him to live here, so that he may keep an inn for the use of pilgrims."

"Why did not Christian and Faithful go there?"

"The city was more dangerous then, and it was not

safe for any of the King's servants to live in it; but now that the people have grown quieter, they have allowed a few good men to build houses in the Fair."

"What can they do in such a place?" said Matthew. "Is it not wrong of them to live there?"

"No. The King has given them work to do for Him even in this wicked city. They help and protect the pilgrims who are passing through it, and when any of them are tempted to stay here, these servants of the King search for them, and try to persuade them to continue their pilgrimage."

"Oh!" said Christiana, "it is comforting to hear of this! We were feeling so frightened, for we thought that the people might put us in prison, or even kill us, as they killed Faithful."

"I am sure they will not kill you," said Greatheart, "and if we pass quietly through the streets they will not try to hinder us."

CHAPTER 29

In Vanity Fair

It was a bright summer evening, and the city looked very beautiful in the light of the setting sun. The buildings were all large and grand, flags fluttered upon the towers and housetops, the people wore rich clothes, and even boys, no older than James and Joseph, were dressed in suits of silk and velvet, and wore large caps with long drooping feathers.

"I should like one of those caps!" whispered Joseph.

Phoebe heard the whisper, and she took the boy's hand in her own. "Don't be foolish, Joseph," she said. "These clothes do not make the boys any happier. The King's clothes are really more beautiful than the brightest of these, and you know you could not be received at the gates of the Heavenly City if you wore clothes belonging to the Wicked Prince."

The town was less busy in the early part of the evening than at any other time of the day. The boys and girls were most of them tired of playing, and lay idly in sunny corners, talking and teasing each other. They laughed at the pilgrims, but they did not crowd round them, or try to prevent their passing through the streets. Even the men and women took very little notice of them. They soon reached the market place

"I should like one of those caps," whispered Joseph.

where Faithful had suffered, and after crossing this wide space, Greatheart led them into a quiet street. He stopped before the house of his friend whose name was Mnason.

Mnason had no sons of his own, and he was always pleased to see Greatheart. "Come in! come in!" he cried. "You know that you are welcome! How far have you traveled today?"

"From the house of Gaius," replied Greatheart. "It has been so hot upon the plain that we are all tired, and will be very glad if you can give us lodging and some food."

"I will give you the best I have," said Mnason; and he led them into a large, cool room, where they could sit quietly and rest while he ordered a meal to be prepared for them.

When the supper was nearly ready, the innkeeper called his eldest daughter, Grace, and asked her to go to the houses of all the King's servants, and tell them that some pilgrims had arrived in the Fair and were staying with him. Grace did so, and presently several of these good people came in, and the evening was spent in talking of the King and of all that He had done for Christiana and her companions.

In the morning Mnason begged Greatheart to remain at his house for a few days. While Greatheart was wondering what to do a message was brought from the King telling the pilgrims to stay in the city for some weeks longer.

Mnason and his two daughters, Grace and Martha,

The girls spent their spare time working for the poor.

were very kind to their guests, and the pilgrims soon found friends among the King's servants. As for old Honesty, Feeble-mind and the lame boy, they were all glad to have a long rest before continuing their journey.

The boys were able to make themselves useful in many ways, and the girls spent their spare time as they had done at the Palace Beautiful in working for the poor.

Although most of the people in Vanity Fair were richly dressed, there were some who had wasted all their money, and were clothed only in rags. These people were very thankful to anyone who would help them. Grace and Martha used to visit many of them, and take them food and clothes, and tell them of the King and His goodness. Christiana and Mercy and Phoebe were glad to help in this good work, so that the days they spent in Vanity Fair were both busy and happy.

The days were both busy and happy.

CHAPTER 30

The Great Dragon

Near to the city of Vanity Fair there was a large forest, and in this forest lived a terrible dragon. It was a fierce and cruel creature, and the people were very much afraid of it. It was so bold that it often came into the midst of the town, and attacked both men and women, and sometimes it even seized children and carried them away to its den. The dragon was called False Teaching, and at times it would cause much damage to those it caught in its evil claws.

The servants of the Wicked Prince hated this dragon almost as much as they hated the King, but none of them were brave enough to resist it. When they heard it roaring, they fled away and tried to hide themselves, so that the savage creature grew more and more bold in its attacks upon the city. The good servants of the King had made up their minds to destroy it if they could, and when they heard that Greatheart was staying at the house of Mnason, they decided to ask him to go out with them.

Greatheart was very willing to help these servants of the King, and one morning a group went forth in search of the dragon. It came out of the forest to meet them, and did not seem to be in the least afraid of them.

It could easily have killed them all.

The Great Dragon

Indeed, it was so strong that it could easily have killed them all, if they had not been armed with the King's weapons. However, they fought against it with all their might, and although they were not able to hurt it much in that first battle, they drove it back into its den, where it lay for several days, angry and frightened, and did not venture to approach the city.

While Greatheart stayed in Vanity Fair, he went out three or four times with the King's servants to fight the dragon, and before he left the city they succeeded in wounding it so that much of its strength and power were lost. The townspeople were very glad when they knew this, and even the wicked men could not help honoring Greatheart and his companions for their bravery.

At last the time came for the pilgrims to continue their journey. Their friends were very sorry to part from them, and gave them many presents.

Grace and Martha, Mnason's two daughters, had been waiting for a guide to take them to the Heavenly City, so their father asked Greatheart whether he would allow them to travel with Christiana. Greatheart answered that he would be pleased to help them.

Many of the King's servants came to the gates of the city of Vanity Fair to bid the pilgrims farewell. Christiana could not help thinking how good the King had been, in letting her meet people who were so kind to her and her companions.

"We might have been treated no better than Christian and Faithful were," she said to Mercy. "I was really very afraid that we would be put in prison, but you see we have found good friends even here, and the King has kept us safely in the middle of this wicked city."

CHAPTER 31

The House in the Valley

The Valley of Peace was only a day's journey from Vanity Fair, and the pilgrims spent the next night in its quiet meadows.

When morning came, Greatheart told Christiana that the King had built a house in this valley where very young pilgrims could be cared for and taught until they were old enough to travel to the Heavenly City.

"Do you mean that I have to leave Innocence there?" asked Christiana.

"It will be wise for you to do so," answered Greatheart. "She is too young to spend all her days in traveling, and you know how hard the path is for her feet."

"But I can carry her," said Christiana.

"Not all the way," said Greatheart, very gently, for he saw tears in the girl's eyes. "I am sure you love Innocence, don't you?"

"Yes."

"The King loves her even more than you do, and He thinks it is better for His little ones to gain strength and wisdom in this quiet valley before they set out on their journey."

"Will I have to go into the Heavenly City without

. . . where very young pilgrims could be cared for.

her? I thought we could all pass through the gates together."

"No. The King generally sends for His pilgrims one by one. Innocence will very likely come to live with you in a place called the Land of Delight; but even if you have to cross the River to the city without her, you need not be troubled, for you may be quite sure that she is safe and happy. I will take you today to see this house which the King has provided."

Poor Christiana felt very sad, but she loved the King too well to disobey Him; and when she had seen the kind women who cared for the very young pilgrims, and the sunny rooms and beautiful gardens in which they lived, she grew more content.

The next day she carried Innocence across the meadows, and led her up the pathway to the door of the King's house. A gentle-looking nurse came out to meet her, and Christiana said, "I have brought my little sister, for Greatheart thinks she is too young to travel any farther with us."

The nurse saw the tears in Christiana's eyes, and she answered, "You do not like to part with her."

"No. I have no other sister, and I thought we could always be together."

"Dear girl!" said the nurse. "I do not wonder that you love her. She will be very happy here, and it will not be long before she is strong enough to follow you."

Then she took Innocence in her arms, and asked Christiana to come into the house with her. Christiana stayed there all day, and in the evening when she had seen Innocence sleeping peacefully in her little bed, she went back again through the valley to the place where the other children were staying.

Greatheart came part of the way to meet her, and he was so kind and gentle that Christiana felt comforted.

"I know the King's servants will teach her better than I can," she said; "and the path is very rough sometimes."

"Yes," replied Greatheart, "and you cannot carry her always. It is right that she should learn to walk alone. When you see her again, you will feel very glad that you trusted her to the care of the King."

Then he told Christiana that the King's Son, the good Prince whom they all loved so dearly, came very often to see the children, and spent much of His time in teaching them and in walking with them in the broad meadows.

"When they are tired, He carries them tenderly in His arms," said Greatheart.

Then Christiana knew deep down that her sister was indeed being well cared for.

CHAPTER 32

Doubting Castle

One day the pilgrims reached a stile which led into By-Path Meadow. There they saw a large stone which Christian and his friend Hopeful had placed by the wayside. The children were tired with walking, for that part of the road was very rough. So they sat down to rest for a while, and soon began to talk about the stone which warned pilgrims of Giant Despair.

"This path leads to Doubting Castle, which belongs to Giant Despair" read the sign. "He is the King's enemy, and he tries to capture pilgrims, but the Key of Promise opens all his locks."

"Why does not someone kill him?" asked Joseph.

"*We* are not strong enough, are we?" said James, looking at Greatheart; "but *you* could kill the biggest giant, couldn't you?"

Greatheart smiled. "Only with the help of the King," he answered; "and the King would help *you* if you trusted in Him."

"So that *we* could kill even Giant Despair?"

"Yes."

"Let us try!" exclaimed Joseph, eagerly. "He was very cruel to Christian!"

"Perhaps there are some pilgrims shut up in the

He had to lie down upon the grass.

castle even now," said Mercy.

"But is it not wrong for us to leave the Way of the King?" asked Christiana.

"If the boys really wish to fight with Giant Despair, the King will not be displeased," answered Greatheart. "Christian and Hopeful went into the meadow for their own pleasure, and that is why they fell into trouble."

"Then do you think we can go?" asked Matthew.

"Yes, if you are ready to fight like brave soldiers."

The boys were only too eager to follow Greatheart to Doubting Castle, and Honesty said that he must certainly go with them. Feeble-mind and Ready-to-halt would not have been able to fight, so they stayed by the wayside with Christiana and the other girls.

Greatheart and his group were soon out of sight, and it was quite late in the day when they returned. They were full of triumph, and brought two poor pilgrims with them, whom they had rescued from the cruel giant. One was an old man, with a sad and weary face. He had been lying for many weeks in a dark dungeon, and even the evening light seemed to dazzle his weak eyes. He looked pale and faint, and when he had been brought safely into the Way of the King, he had to lie down upon the grass, while Christiana and her friends rubbed his cold hands, and fed him with wholesome food.

Presently he revived a little, and was able to sit up and thank his deliverers. He told them that his name was Despondency, and that he had been traveling to the Heavenly City with his daughter Much-afraid. The poor girl had done her best to comfort her father in his distress, but they had both lost all hope of being saved, and could scarcely believe that Greatheart was a servant of the King, and that they were really free once more.

"Did you kill the giant?" whispered Mercy to Matthew.

"Yes, and his wife too. She was very cruel, and she deserved to die as well as her husband. Oh, Mercy, the castle was such a dreadful place!"

"I am glad *we* did not fall into the giant's hands," said Mercy. "That poor girl looks as if she might die even now."

"She will soon grow stronger if we take care of her."

"Did you destroy the castle?"

"We broke down all the gates and doors."

"You must have been frightened by the giant."

"He was very rough and savage, but we prayed to the King, and even Joseph fought bravely. It was our first real battle!" Matthew's eyes shone as he put his sword back into its sheath. There would be further battles on the path ahead!

CHAPTER 33

The Delectable Mountains

Greatheart had now quite a large party of pilgrims under his care. Honesty took charge of Despondency; and Much-afraid, although she was older than the other girls, was very glad of their pleasant company.

The Shepherds, who lived upon the Delectable Mountains, were always busy with their sheep. When they saw the pilgrims coming toward their tents, they were very pleased to find that Greatheart was with them. All the King's servants knew and loved him, for he was such a gentle and faithful guide.

It was a clear, bright night, but as Despondency and his daughter were so weak after their long imprisonment, Greatheart thought it wise to remain with the Shepherds until the next day.

These men welcomed the whole party to their tents, and gave them food and prepared beds for them, so that in the morning they rose up refreshed and strengthened.

The Shepherds were always very glad when any of the King's pilgrims came to stay with them. They liked to take their visitors up to see the view of the Heavenly City, and the many strange places upon the mountains.

Christiana and her friends enjoyed their walk upon

She caught a glimpse of the Heavenly City.

The Delectable Mountains

the hills very much. When she was sitting on the highest hill, Christiana looked into the distance. There, shining brightly on the distant hills, she caught a glimpse of the Heavenly City. When they had seen all the wonderful sights, there was still a little time to spare before they continued their journey. So, instead of turning back to the tents, the Shepherds led the pilgrims to a very beautiful hill called Mount Innocence.

Not far from where they stood, a man was walking upon the green slope. He was clothed in white, and his garments had not a single spot or stain upon them. But while the pilgrims watched him, two other men came across the mountain, and when they saw the man's white robes, they filled their hands with earth, and began to pelt him with it.

"Oh," cried the children, "they will spoil his clothes!"

"No," said the Shepherds, "the King will prevent that."

And, as the man came nearer, the pilgrims saw that the dirt, although it struck his clothes, fell from them without leaving the slightest stain.

"There is a lesson in that!" said Honesty.

"Yes," said Greatheart, "a very good lesson for all the King's pilgrims. When wicked people speak evil of them, they need not be unhappy, for the King will not allow false words to do them any real harm."

"And you may remember also," said the Shepherds, "that it is only by your own fault that the clothes which the King gives you can be stained. None of your enemies has any power to spoil them."

Christiana's Journey

After this the Shepherds took their visitors to Mount Charity. A good man lived there, whose work was to provide clothes for some of the King's servants who were very poor indeed. He showed the pilgrims a wonderful roll of cloth which the King had given him to use. Every day he cut from it as many garments as were needed, and yet the cloth never came to an end.

"It is very strange!" said Christiana, as she watched the man at his work.

"The King's power and goodness are so wonderful!" said the Shepherds. "Those who really try to help His poor servants may be sure that their stores will never fail."

Soon the young pilgrims came upon two children washing a black lamb. The more the lamb was washed, the blacker it seemed. The two children were called Stupidity and Blindness.

"What are they trying to do?" asked Mercy.

Honesty shook his head sadly. "They are too stupid to be able to see that they can never wash a black lamb white. The more they try, the more the blackness shows."

"So it is with us," agreed Greatheart. "We can never make ourselves clean. We must let the Prince Himself wash us to make us ready for meeting the King in the Heavenly City."

"I am sure that He has made all of *us* clean," said Christiana, "because we all belong to the King now. I *know* that He will receive us!"

CHAPTER 34

The Wonderful Glass

Although the Shepherds lived in tents during the summer, they had also a large house which the King had given into their care. It was to be used as a place of rest for His pilgrims. When the children returned from their walk upon the mountains, they found a meal prepared for them in this house. As soon as they had eaten, Greatheart desired them to get ready for their journey.

Mercy had eaten very little, and she looked so pale and sad that Christiana whispered, "What is the matter, Mercy? Are you ill?"

Tears came into Mercy's eyes, but she shook her head, and said nothing.

"What is it?" asked Christiana. "Tell me what is troubling you."

"It isn't right for me to wish for things," said Mercy, "but you have your beautiful anchor, and I saw something just now that I should *so* like to have!"

"What did you see? Perhaps it is something that we may ask for."

"It is a small looking-glass in the dining room. I looked at it before the meal. You can see yourself in it, but when you turn it round, you don't see yourself any more, but our dear Prince instead. It is so beautiful! There is the crown of thorns upon His head, and He seemed to smile at me, and I feel as if I could not be happy unless I had it."

Christiana understood how Mercy felt. "The Shepherds are very kind," she said. "Perhaps if they knew you wished for it, they would be willing to let us have it."

"I could buy it, you know," said Mercy; "I have a little money."

"Well, don't cry any more. I will go now and ask the Shepherds about it."

So Mercy dried her tears, and after a few minutes a Shepherd called Experience came toward her. He spoke very gently, and laid his hand kindly on Mercy's shoulder. "Christiana says that you have seen something in our house that you would like to have for your own. Tell me what it is, and the King will be very glad for us to give it to you."

Mercy blushed, but she looked up at the Shepherd and answered, "It is the glass in the dining room, in which you can see the Prince."

When he heard what Mercy said, Experience went at once into the house, and brought out the glass. Mercy scarcely knew what to say when it was placed in her hands, but the Shepherds saw how shy she was, and they understood quite well that she was too happy and grateful for many words.

Then these men brought out of their treasures a present for each of the travelers, and after wishing them a pleasant journey, they watched the pilgrims until all were out of sight.

CHAPTER 35

Mr. Valiant

When Christian and Hopeful had been on their journey, Christian told his friend the story of Little-faith, who had foolishly lain down to sleep by the wayside, and had been robbed by some wicked boys. Greatheart and the pilgrims now came to the very place where Little-faith had slept. It was at the corner of a lane, which led out from the Way of the King directly into the country of the Wicked Prince.

As they drew near, they saw a man standing alone, with his sword in his hand, and his armor stained with blood. Greatheart stopped and asked him what had happened. The man was tall and strong, with a brave face. As Christiana looked at him, she felt sure that she had seen him before.

"My name is Valiant," he answered, "and I am a pilgrim. Three men came down this lane and attacked me as I was passing. They said I must take my choice of three things: to join them in robbing the King's pilgrims, to go back to my own city, or to be put to death on this spot."

"What did you say to them?" asked Greatheart.

"I told them that I had always tried to be honest, and I certainly would not become a thief now; and that, as for

141

"They drew their swords, and I drew mine."

my own city, I would not have left it if I had been happy there. It was a bad place, and I had forsaken it forever. Then they asked me if I wished to lose my life, and I said my life was worth too much for me to give it up lightly, and that they had no right to treat the King's servants in such a manner. So they drew their swords, and I drew mine, and we have been fighting for nearly three hours. They have wounded me, but I think I wounded them also. I suppose they must have heard your steps in the distance, for they suddenly turned and fled away, and then I saw you coming."

"That was a hard battle, three men to one," said Greatheart.

"Yes," replied Valiant; "but I knew I was fighting against my King's enemies, and that gave me courage."

"Did you not cry for help? Some of the King's servants might have been near enough to hear you."

"I cried to the King Himself, and I am sure He answered me. I could not have fought so long in my own strength."

Greatheart smiled. "You are one of our King's true servants! Let me see your sword. Ah, yes, this is from the right armory!"

"It is a good sword," said Valiant. "No man who has so fine a weapon need be afraid, if he has learned how to use it skillfully."

"And you fought for three hours?" said Greatheart. "Were you not ready to faint with fatigue?"

"No, as I fought, my sword clung to my hand, as if it were a part of my arm; and I think that made me feel stronger."

Christiana's Journey

"You have been very brave!" answered Greatheart. "You must finish your journey with us. We shall all be glad of your company."

Honesty, Despondency and the children all joined in welcoming the brave soldier. Christiana washed his wounds, and Mercy and Phoebe helped her to bind them up. After this they brought him food, and made him rest for a little while. Then, as the evening was coming on, they started once more on their journey.

CHAPTER 36

Christian's Father

Christiana was walking just behind Greatheart and Valiant, so she could hear all that the soldier said in answer to the questions of the young guide. She was still wondering where she had seen him before, when she heard him say that he had once lived in the City of Destruction.

"What made you become a pilgrim?" asked Greatheart.

"I had a son," replied Valiant; "and when he knew that his mother had gone to live with the King, he never rested until he had found out how to follow her. He went away one morning, and we did not miss him until it was too late for us to stop him and bring him back."

"What was his name?" asked Greatheart; and Christiana listened eagerly for the answer, for she felt sure now that she knew who the soldier was.

"My son's name was Christian," he answered. "I was very grieved when I heard what had happened, and it was many months before we had any certain news of him. Then a man named Truth came to our city, and he met me one day, and told me how my brave boy had traveled safely along the Way of the King and had reached the Dark River, and crossed it, and had been received by the angels at the gates of the Heavenly City. Truth told me also that the boy and his mother were living happily in the presence of the King, and when I heard this I began to feel restless and sad. Serving the Wicked Prince was no longer pleasant to me, and I forsook him and became a pilgrim."

"Did you come in at the Gate to the King's Way?" asked Greatheart.

"Yes, for Truth had told me that I could not be received by the King unless I did so."

Greatheart turned round and looked at Christiana with a smile.

"You see," he said, "the King has fulfilled Christian's wish."

Then Valiant turned also. "Did you know my boy?" he asked.

Christiana answered with a happy smile, for she knew how Christian had longed for his father to follow him.

"Ah!" said Valiant; "it will give him great pleasure when he looks out through the gates of the Heavenly City, and finds so many of his friends are waiting to enter!"

Greatheart and the soldier went on talking for some time, and Christiana listened to Valiant's account of his pilgrimage. He had always been very brave, and careful in his work, so that his master, the Wicked Prince, had been very unwilling to lose so good a servant. Valiant's friends had done everything they could to keep him in the City of Destruction, and they had tried to frighten him by telling him of the dangers he would meet with if he became a pilgrim. They told him of the fierce giants, and the lions, and the Hill Difficulty, of the Enchanted Ground, and the net of the Flatterer, and of the Dark River, over which there was no bridge, and which must be passed before he could enter the Heavenly City. They reminded him also of the many pilgrims who had returned to their homes after having a look at the Way of the King. They also declared that the story of his son's happiness was not a true one, for they said that they knew he had certainly been lost in the Dark River, and had never reached the opposite shore at all!

"Did not all these things discourage you?" asked Greatheart.

"No," replied Valiant. "I felt that Truth could not possibly be deceiving me, so I left the city and began my journey."

"And you have not been sorry?"

"No, indeed! I have met with many enemies, but I have trusted in the King, and He has helped me to conquer them all!"

CHAPTER 37

The Enchanted Ground

"We have now come to the Enchanted Ground," warned Greatheart suddenly. "We must all be sure to stay wide awake!"

Although the Enchanted Ground was a pleasant place, in which pilgrims were tempted to rest after the toils of their journey, they sometimes found the path across it full of difficulty and trouble.

The air was so warm and still that it made everyone feel sleepy, and the servants of the Wicked Prince had built many shelters in the hope that foolish pilgrims would lie down to rest in them, and so fall sleepily into the hands of the enemy. They had also planted a number of brambles close to the Way of the King, and these had flourished so well that their long prickly branches were trailing all over the pathway, and Christiana and her companions had to pick their way among them very carefully indeed.

There had been a heavy storm of rain in the early morning, which had left the path soft and wet, so that with the mud and the thorns the pilgrims began to feel weary and discouraged.

Greatheart and Valiant did their best to cheer the tired children. Greatheart went first, and made Feeble-mind lean upon his arm. Valiant came last of all, leading Much-afraid, who was still weak from being kept for so long by Giant Despair.

Soon they passed by a large and very beautiful shelter, and if the children had been alone they might have been tempted to enter it. The walls were neatly made, and the roof had been covered that morning with fresh, green leafy branches which made it look cool and pleasant. But the pilgrims had learned to trust their wise young guide, and he had warned them that they must not think of sleeping until they had safely crossed this dangerous countryside.

Night came on while they were in the midst of the Enchanted Ground, and this made traveling more difficult, for the air was damp and foggy, and the moon was not shining. However, Greatheart led them slowly along, and presently he told them to stand still for a few minutes.

"We are coming to a place where several paths lead out of the Way of the King," said he; "and it is so dark I must look carefully at my map, or we may turn off this road and be lost."

He struck a light and drew out his map, and as he looked before him at the path, he saw a great pit filled with mud. Wicked soldiers had dug this just where the pilgrims would have to pass, so that if they had gone on in the darkness some of them would have been sure to fall into it, and might have been covered before anyone could have drawn them out.

Not far from the pit was another shelter, and in it lay

The Enchanted Ground

two pilgrims, sleeping soundly. They were lads about Matthew's age, and as Greatheart looked at them he said, "We must try to waken them."

But although Greatheart called them by their names, for he knew who they were, they did not hear him, and at last he took them by the shoulders and shook them. This roused them a little, and one of them murmured, "I will pay you when I get some money," and the other said, "I will fight as long as I can hold a sword." Then they settled themselves to sleep again.

Greatheart turned away, for he saw that they could not be awakened.

"What did they mean?" asked Christiana.

"They did not know what they were saying," he answered. "They are in the power of the Wicked Prince, and he will not let them understand their danger, until it is too late for them to escape from it. Perhaps the King will send someone who is specially able to help them. I will ask Him to do so."

CHAPTER 38

Another Pilgrim

It was now so dark that the pilgrims could scarcely find their way, so they begged Greatheart to light his lantern. With this to guide and cheer them, they traveled more comfortably, but the girls and the two youngest boys were growing very tired, and they began to pray to the King to help them in their weariness.

Presently a cool, fresh breeze sprang up, and the air became clearer. Although the moon was still hidden by the clouds, the children could now see each other as they walked along.

"Have we nearly crossed the Enchanted Ground?" asked Christiana.

"Not yet," replied Greatheart; "but this is your last night of trouble. Tomorrow we shall reach the Land of Delight, and you will be able to rest there without fear of danger."

"When do we go into the Heavenly City?" asked James.

"I do not know," answered Greatheart. "The King may send for you very soon, or He may give you work to do for Him in the Land of Delight, or He may perhaps send you to help other pilgrims on their journey, as He has sent me."

"To be guides, and fight giants, as you have done for

Standfast was talking to the King.

us?" asked Joseph eagerly.

"Perhaps, when you are older," said Greatheart, smiling; "but I cannot tell you what the King may think best for you. I only know that you will be happy, so that whatever He desires you to do for Him, you will love to do it."

Before the sun rose, while the sky was still dark, the pilgrims heard a sound of someone speaking, not very far from them. They went on quietly, and soon they saw a boy upon his knees by the wayside, with his face turned toward the sky. They knew that he was talking to the King, but as he did not seem to hear their steps, they walked slowly, so that they would not disturb him. In a few moments he got up, and began to run on towards the Heavenly City. But Greatheart, seeing that he was a pilgrim, called to him to wait for them.

"Ah!" said old Honesty, when the lad turned round, "I know him!"

"Do you?" asked Valiant. "Who is he?"

"He comes from my own city," replied Honesty. "His name is Standfast, and he is one of the King's true pilgrims."

Standfast caught sight of the old man. "What, Honesty!" he cried. "Are *you* a pilgrim, too?"

"Yes, indeed," replied Honesty.

"It does me good to see you!" said the lad, grasping his hand.

"And it did me good to see you seeking the help of your King like a faithful servant," replied Honesty.

"Have you been in danger?" asked Valiant; "or were

you praising the King for His mercies?"

"I was in danger," answered Standfast, and then he told his new friends what had happened to him.

CHAPTER 39

Folly

The Wicked Prince knew that when the pilgrims reached the Land of Delight he would no longer be able to trouble them. So he employed very many of his people in tempting the King's servants while they were still upon this part of their journey.

Standfast told the pilgrims he had been met by a girl whose name was Folly. She was very pretty, and had a pleasant way of talking.

"You look very tired," she said to him, "and I am sure you must be lonely. Let me walk with you and be your friend."

But she was not wearing the King's clothes and Standfast knew by her way of talking that she was not a pilgrim, and he would have nothing to say to her. He walked on silently, and she walked beside him, smiling and saying pleasant things, until at last he grew angry, and told her not to trouble him.

When she heard his angry words she laughed and bade him follow her. "I will teach you how to be really happy," she said, "if you will promise to do what I tell you."

But Standfast would not listen to her, and when he found that she was determined not to leave him, he knelt down upon the road, and prayed the King to deliver him from following her.

"I felt sure the King would help me," said Standfast. "He did so by letting you find me just at the right moment. I did not hear your steps, but the girl must have seen you, for she suddenly turned and went away. Then I thanked the King for His goodness, and I was going to hurry on my way when I heard you call to me."

"I believe I have seen that girl," said Honesty," or perhaps I have read of her in one of the King's books."

"You may have done both," said Standfast. "She told me her name was Folly."

"Ah!" replied Honesty. "She is tall, is she not, and her eyes and hair are dark?"

"Yes," said Standfast.

"She smiles when she speaks, and she has a purse filled with gold. She is always turning over the money with her fingers as if she loved to touch it."

"Yes, she is just like that."

"I thought I knew something of her. She is a very dangerous enemy."

"Indeed she is," said Greatheart. "Although she is so young, she does more mischief upon the Enchanted Ground than any other of the Wicked Prince's servants. She spends most of her time here, but she is sometimes met with near the Gate and tries to hinder people who are looking for the Way of the King. I could tell you many sad stories of pilgrims who have been deceived by her."

"I saw that she was not a good companion," said

Folly

Standfast; "but I did not know that I was in such great
danger."

"Bad companions are always dangerous," replied
Greatheart. "You did well to pray to the King, for you
would have found it difficult to escape from her."

CHAPTER 40

A Happy Morning

The sun had now risen, and the pilgrims saw before them, in the soft light, the beautiful hills which lay beyond the Dark River. The river itself was not in sight, and they could not yet see the glory of the Heavenly City. But they knew that the golden gates were not very far away, and that when they had entered the Land of Delight, all the trouble and danger of their pilgrimage would be over.

"I am glad I came with you!" whispered Mercy to Christiana. "I have often been very frightened, but now I am happy."

"Yes," said Christiana, "we could never have been so happy in our old home."

Then she looked round at her brothers. Matthew had grown taller, and his face was more thoughtful, and the change in him pleased his sister.

"I think Matthew will be a little like Greatheart in a year or two, don't you?" she said.

"Perhaps the King will give him the same work to do," suggested Mercy.

"To guide the pilgrims? Ah, that is the best work of all. If he could ever be wise enough!"

Christiana's Journey

"Do you think Greatheart was wise at first? He must have been taught, or he could not know so much about the King and His will. And Matthew is kind and careful—he would be a good guide."

"Perhaps he would," said Christiana. "He is very brave now that he really loves the King."

James and Joseph were tired after so much traveling, but the journey had done them good, and their strong figures were good to see. Then Christiana thought of Innocence in the Valley of Peace, and wondered how long it would be before she joined them in this sunny Land of Delight.

All the pilgrims were quiet and thoughtful as they left the plain, and followed Greatheart along the sheltered pathways of this beautiful country. Feeble-mind clung closer than ever to Greatheart, for he was still timid at the sight of strange faces. When the people of the land saw the pilgrims they came out to welcome them.

Despondency had found a good friend in Valiant; and Much-afraid, though she seldom left her father's side, generally had one of the elder girls for her companion. Christiana and Mercy were never far apart, and the two youngest boys looked upon good-natured old Honesty as their special friend. So they took the last steps of their journey together, and presently found themselves in one of the King's vineyards, where Greatheart told them to rest.

"We were so few when we started," said Mercy, as she nestled down upon the soft grass, with her hand

A Happy Morning

round Christiana's arm. "Now we are quite a large company! Some young and some old, some weak and some strong, and yet the King has cared for us all!"

CHAPTER 41

In the Land of Delight

The pilgrims were very happy in the Land of Delight. The King's servants provided homes for them all, and told them what work needed to be done. Despondency and Feeble-mind had only to rest quietly until the King sent for them, but the younger ones had each their own duties to perform.

Christiana spent much of her time in teaching James and Joseph, and she often went with others of the King's servants to welcome the new pilgrims who came into the country nearly every day. Sometimes she slipped quietly away with Mercy to walk by the side of the Dark River. The sight of the troubled waters made Mercy tremble, but Christiana always looked beyond them at the beautiful golden light. At last Mercy began to lose her fear, and she tried to feel as Christiana did. She knew that the coming of the King's messenger would be the beginning of a greater happiness than any she had yet known.

"If only the water were less dark and rough," Mercy would say, "or if I could have *you* to cross with me, Christiana. But if I go alone it will be dreadful!"

"You should not think of the water at all," Christiana always answered. "You should think of the glorious

City, and the King who lives there, and our Prince, and of the angels who will receive you. Oh, Mercy, you need not be afraid!"

But although her fear grew less, Mercy never liked to watch the river. She loved best to wander in the King's gardens, and talk to the children who spent so many hours among the vines and flowers. One duty which the King desired even the youngest children to perform was the gathering of flowers every day for the older pilgrims, especially for those who were *very* old and weak, and not able to walk in the gardens and enjoy the beauty and perfume of the growing blossoms.

Old Honesty often met them in the gardens in the early morning, and he used to say, "We old pilgrims are very happy, for the young pilgrims cover our way with flowers."

In one of the houses a book was kept, in which the King's servants had written the names of many pilgrims who had crossed the river, and the stories of their lives. Matthew and his new friend Standfast studied this book very carefully, and hoped that the King would some day allow them to fight for Him as bravely as the soldiers of whom they read.

The lame boy, Ready-to-halt, loved the book too, but his favorite stories were those of pilgrims who had been weak like himself.

"There are so many!" he said one day. "I think it is very comforting to read about them."

Even Despondency seemed more cheerful when Ready-to-halt came to see him, and told him of the King's love for the weak pilgrims.

CHAPTER 42

Christiana Crosses the River

Greatheart was glad he had brought Christiana and her companions safely to their journey's end. When he returned to his master's house, he had promised that he would some day visit them again. Most of his time was spent in guiding pilgrims along the Way of the King.

At last the day came for Innocence to leave the Valley of Peace. Her kind nurses sent for Greatheart, and desired him to take the child safely to her sister. Innocence had learned to love her nurses, but she had not forgotten either Christiana or the young guide. She went with Greatheart quite contentedly, and it would be difficult to say which of the two received the warmer welcome when they reached Christiana's new home!

Greatheart himself was very pleased to see the pilgrims again, and he told them that his master had given him permission to stay with them in the Land of Delight for a few weeks, so that he might rest in the King's gardens, and prepare himself for future work.

When these weeks of rest were over, it pleased the King to give Greatheart some work to do in the Land of Delight, but before this was finished, Christiana and several of the older pilgrims had to cross the Dark

Christiana and Mercy at the Dark River.

Christiana Crosses the River

River and enter the Heavenly City.

Christiana and Mercy had often watched the King's messengers as they passed through the streets, and wondered at whose house they would knock, and when at last an angel was seen standing at their own door, the two girls trembled with a mixture of both fear and joy.

But the message was not for Mercy. The angel spoke to Christiana.

"Our King calls for you," he said. "He wishes you to come to His Palace."

Christiana felt glad to think of being with the King in His glorious City, but she was sorry to leave her brothers and Innocence, and all her kind friends. However, she knew that it would not be very long before they followed her, and when she remembered this it comforted her.

She thought she would like to bid Greatheart goodby, so she sent for him, and told him what the angel had said; and he stayed with her a little while, talking about the River and the way of crossing it.

When the other pilgrims heard that Christiana was going away, they came to see her also. She asked Valiant to be a friend to her brothers and sister, and he promised that he would watch over them as long as he remained in that country.

Then she bade them all goodby, but they would not let her go away alone. They came with her to the water's edge, and watched her until she was out of sight. They could see angels waiting on the other side,

Christiana's Journey

and they knew when Christiana had safely reached the shore for the bright company moved slowly away from the River up the steep pathway to the golden gates, and disappeared at last in the glory of the Heavenly City.

Poor Innocence cried when her sister left her, and so did James and Joseph, but Matthew and Mercy took them home and comforted them.

Greatheart and Valiant could not be sad, although they both loved Christiana dearly. They knew that she had entered the Heavenly City, and that she would never be weary or anxious any more; so, instead of weeping, they praised the King who had taken His faithful pilgrim to dwell with Him forever.

CHAPTER 43

The King Calls for His Servants

It was not long after the departure of Christiana that a message was brought to the lame boy, Ready-to-halt. Valiant and Greatheart were both with him when he received the King's summons. He turned to Valiant, saying, "You must keep my crutches until you find another lame pilgrim, and then give them to him with my good wishes, and tell him that I hope he will be able to serve the King better than I have done."

Then he looked at Greatheart and said, "You have been very kind to me, and you have helped me wonderfully in my pilgrimage!"

His two friends went with him to the brink of the River, and when he had stepped into the water, he laid his crutches down upon the bank.

"I shall never use them again!" he said; "I know that in the King's City there are horses and chariots which shine like the sun. But I will not need to ride them, for the King Himself will heal me and make me strong!"

A few days later Feeble-mind was sent for. The King's message to him was very kind and gentle, and the pilgrim rejoiced to think that he would soon be in a land where toil and trouble are unknown.

Some time passed before any angels came again, and

their next message was for Despondency. When Much-afraid heard it she begged to go with him, and the King, who knew how dearly she loved her father, and how faithful she had been to him through all the dangers and difficulties of their pilgrimage, granted her request. So the father and daughter entered the Dark River hand in hand, and the pilgrims upon the shore could hear Much-afraid singing a song of praise as she went through the water, although she was too far away for them to distinguish its words.

Honesty received the next summons, and just at that time the River was so full of water that it overflowed its banks. But, although it seemed terribly wide and deep, the old man was not afraid. He knew that his King would not allow him to perish in the dark waters. He went cheerfully down to the shore at the appointed time, and there he found a friend waiting for him—a man whom he had known nearly all his life, whose name was Good-conscience.

He had once said to him, "I hope to have your help when I cross the Dark River," and Good-conscience had remembered this, and had obtained the King's permission to help his friend in this last hour of trouble. So he gave him his hand; and although the waters raged wildly around them, Honesty leaned upon his strong shoulders, and crossed the River in safety.

CHAPTER 44

The Departure of Valiant and Standfast

The same messenger who called Honesty summoned Christian's father, Valiant, and he went over the River later in the day. He had no fear of the crossing, for he had always been brave, and his heart was full of trust in the good King. He was longing to see his wife and his son once more; and he knew how happy Christian and his mother would be when they heard who was crossing the river.

"Mine has been a hard pilgrimage," he said, "and I have had to fight through many troubles and dangers, but I am going now to my true home in the Heavenly City where I shall be safe and happy forever."

The good soldier had no longer any use for his sword, so he left the bright weapon in Greatheart's care and asked him to give it to some other pilgrim. Then he entered the River, and his friends soon lost sight of him, but presently the sound of the silver trumpets was heard upon the other shore, and they knew that Valiant was on his way to the gates of the City.

Standfast, who was now Matthew's closest friend, had hoped that he might be allowed to spend a long life in working for the King, but this was not his Master's

173

The welcome to the Heavenly City.

will. The King had need of His faithful young servant in the Heavenly City, and he was summoned to cross the River.

At first Standfast could scarcely believe that the King really wished to receive him into His own Palace, but the angel assured him that it was true.

"You have served my Master very faithfully," he said, "but He is not willing that you should be living at a distance from Him any longer."

So Standfast prepared for his last journey, and gave Greatheart many messages, for he hoped that the guide would perhaps some day meet with others of his family who might be following in his steps. The floods had gone down, and the water was very still and calm; so that when Standfast reached the middle of the River, he turned and spoke once more to his friends.

"This River makes so many people afraid!" he said. "Indeed, I was frightened myself before I entered it. But my fear is all gone; I can feel the firm ground under my feet, and very soon I shall be with my Prince. It has been very pleasant to hear of Him and think of Him, but now I shall see Him with my own eyes. He has helped me and strengthened me all through my pilgrimage and He is with me now!"

Then the other pilgrims saw that as he turned again toward the City, a beautiful light fell upon his face. In the clear air they could see across the River and were able to watch the multitude of angels who came down to receive the faithful pilgrim, and lead him into the presence of the King.

Christiana's Journey

Christian, standing in the Heavenly City with his mother and father, turned to Christiana as they watched. Then they began to sing a beautiful song of praise to their King. Soon all the people joined in with them until it seemed that the whole Heavenly City was alive with music and praise. Everyone cried out,

"Praise the Lord. For the Lord our God, the Almighty, reigns. Let us be glad and rejoice and honour Him."

And over the Dark River flew a white Dove. Christian and Christiana knew this was the Spirit of the King Himself, saying,

"Do not be afraid. My Son is the Way to the Heavenly City!"